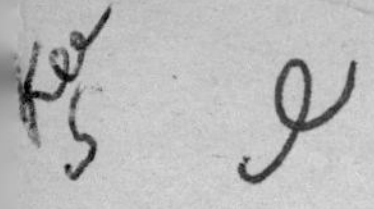

"TONIGHT, I FINALLY LIVED OUT MY DREAM," STEPHEN WHISPERED.

"For years I've fantasized about making love to you. I never forgot how it felt to kiss you so many years ago."

Jane felt a chill run through her and she pulled away from his firm hold. Was he feeling triumphant because he'd finally made love to his teenage fantasy? "Please don't say that!" she cried. "Don't you know that I'm a flesh-and-blood woman? I'm far from perfect. I make mistakes. I'm not the goddess you've created in your memory!"

Stephen reached out for her with concern. "Of course I know you're not a fantasy. It's *you* I want, Jane. You're the woman I love—"

But she shook her head, her eyes filled with tears. "Why are you so blind? This will never work between us. Can't you see that it's someone else you love and not me at all?"

CANDLELIGHT ECSTASY ROMANCES®

410 SWEET-TIME LOVIN', *Blair Cameron*
411 SING SOFTLY TO ME, *Dorothy Phillips*
412 ALL A MAN COULD WANT, *Linda Randall Wisdom*
413 SOMETHING WILD AND FREE, *Helen Conrad*
414 TO THE HIGHEST BIDDER, *Neva Beach*
415 HANDS OFF THE LADY, *Elise Randolph*
416 WITH EVERY KISS, *Sheila Paulos*
417 DREAM MAKER, *Donna Kimel Vitek*
418 GYPSY RENEGADE, *Megan Lane*
419 A HINT OF SPLENDOR, *Kathy Clark*
420 DOCTOR'S ORDERS, *Paula Hamilton*
421 RACE THE WIND, *Jackie Lyons*
422 FORTUNE HUNTER, *Cory Kenyon*
423 A WOMAN'S TOUCH, *Karen Whittenburg*
424 MIDNIGHT SECRETS, *Kit Daley*
425 TONIGHT YOU'RE MINE, *Edith Delatush*

FANTASY LOVER

Anne Silverlock

A Candlelight Ecstasy Romance®

Published by
Dell Publishing Co., Inc.
1 Dag Hammarskjold Plaza
New York, New York 10017

ISBN: 0-440-12438-7

Printed in the United States of America

May 1986
10 9 8 7 6 5 4 3 2 1
WFH

To Our Readers:

We have been delighted with your enthusiastic response to Candlelight Ecstasy Romances®, and we thank you for the interest you have shown in this exciting series.

In the upcoming months we will continue to present the distinctive, sensuous love stories you have come to expect only from Ecstasy. We look forward to bringing you many more books from your favorite authors and also the very finest work from new authors of contemporary romantic fiction.

As always, we are striving to present the unique, absorbing love stories that you enjoy most—books that are more than ordinary romance.

Your suggestions and comments are always welcome. Please write to us at the address below.

Sincerely,

The Editors
Candlelight Romances
1 Dag Hammarskjold Plaza
New York, New York 10017

FANTASY LOVER

PROLOGUE

Ten Years Before the Story Begins

It was silly to be depressed about the end of summer school. Nevertheless, Janie was feeling kind of low. While her fingers unconsciously tugged on the small silver pendant she wore around her neck, her eyes searched the room for Stephen. He was the one who'd talked her into coming to this noisy, last-night-of-the-semester bash.

Across the tiny apartment jammed with a motley assortment of celebrating students, she caught sight of him. He was carrying on an animated conversation with one of his crazy new pals. Though he'd been on Skyler's campus only a few weeks, he seemed to know everyone. Whereas Janie, who'd been a student here for two years, had only a few select friends.

Stephen, whom Janie had met in her music theory class and who lived across from her residence hall, was now one of those friends. Her large blue eyes warmed as she watched him.

Of course he wasn't her date or anything. He was too young for her, and she already had a fiancé—Ward Cowle—and he'd just graduated from law school. Because Ward was vacationing in Europe with his parents, Janie had been left pretty much on her own this summer. That's why she and Stephen were spending so much time together. He was a friendly kid, and she'd enjoyed their camaraderie. He'd come East for the summer just to participate in a special music program at Skyler and was away from his home in California for the first time. When they first met he'd been lonely too.

A few moments later he strolled over and crouched down beside her. She could see he'd had a couple of beers, which was unusual for him. His shirttail was hanging out of his well-worn jeans and his thatch of curly dark hair stuck out over his ears as if he'd been combing it with agitated fingers. Amused, she watched as he arranged his lanky body in a cross-legged position, spilling some of the beer out of the can he held as he struggled with his long legs.

"So how do you like the party?" he asked.

"Not very much. I don't know many of the people here."

Stephen wrapped his fingers around the base of his beer can. "Me neither."

"Then why did you want to come?" Janie lifted a golden eyebrow. Stephen could be the most puzzling person. Usually he had a disposition that was like a dose of sunshine. But for the past couple of days he'd been moody and unpredictable.

He didn't look at her when he answered. Instead, he stared down at the floor. "Oh, I don't know. It's the last day. Tomorrow I'll be going back home, and you'll be staying here. We might never see each other again, so I thought we ought to do something."

"We could have done something together," Janie pointed out. They always had a good time when it was just the two of them. And they'd had a lot of good times over the past eight weeks. There'd been expeditions to the farmers' market to buy fresh honey, and free concerts, and just sitting on the front porch of Stephen's rooming house talking about everything and nothing.

"It's been fun, hasn't it?" he said, looking up to watch her intently.

"Yes it has," she agreed. "I'm going to miss you."

"I'm going to miss you too." There was a catch in his voice and he looked away for a moment. "Janie," he suddenly blurted. "There's another reason why I wanted to come to this party instead of doing something just the two of us."

She cocked her head curiously, wondering what he was going to say.

"It was because I wanted to be with you tonight, and I was afraid if we were alone, I'd say something dumb."

"Like what?"

He looked at her then, and between his black lashes his dark eyes were filled with an emotion that made her uneasy. "Like this." He took a deep breath. "Janie, I know you think you're in love with this guy Ward, and you're dropping out of school to marry him. But you're making a big mistake. You're not ready for marriage yet. Forget about him and come back to California with me."

She was dumbfounded. "What? Stephen, are you crazy?"

Now that he'd started his incredible proposition, he went on in a rush, his words tumbling over themselves. "You can finish school out there. We can live together—just as friends if that's the way you want it. We're both musicians; we understand each other. You'll be happier with me than with your lawyer.

And," he added urgently, "you can count on me. I'd walk through fire before I'd ever let you down."

Janie continued to gape at him. The offer was totally unexpected. They were just buddies. Stephen hadn't even kissed her! And now he was asking her to go all the way across the continent to live with him when he knew she was already engaged? Her first impulse was to laugh out loud. He was a year younger than her worldly-wise twenty and she viewed him indulgently, as if he were a likable but rather harum-scarum younger brother. The idea of leaving school and deserting Ward to fly off to California with Stephen Hammond was simply ludicrous.

Then she smiled. She caught a whiff of the beer he'd downed. Stephen wasn't used to drinking. Obviously it was the alcohol talking. He would feel pretty silly when he remembered this in the morning—if he remembered it. Janie grinned and patted his knee affectionately.

"I think you've had too much beer. We've been very special friends, but I'm engaged—remember?"

For a long moment he stared expressionlessly at her. Then, without a word, he jumped to his feet and strode away.

Stephen avoided her for the rest of the evening, and when he finally walked Janie home he was aloof, speaking only when she asked a question but otherwise not saying anything at all. It was after midnight when they rounded the corner of the block where her dormitory was located. Across the street from it, they stood in front of his rooming house, the awkward silence continuing to stretch between them.

"Stephen, what's wrong?" she finally asked.

He looked down at his feet. "I feel awful," he muttered. He had his hands jammed in his pockets, and a bleak look on his face.

"I bet you do," she said dryly. "You shouldn't have had all that beer. You know you're not a drinker."

"It's not that." He wandered over to a tree and leaned against it. "Janie, I know you don't want to hear this, but I'm going to say it anyway. Don't marry Ward Cowle. Wait for me."

"Wait for you?" Her words caught in her throat.

He started to walk toward her. "Yes, wait for me. I have to go home now, but I'll be back if you say the word."

"But, Stephen . . ." Dismayed, she fingered the small pendant which hung at her throat and looked up at the sky. It was a warm night, and there was a full moon. It shed a silvery radiance over the scene, reinforcing the sense of unreality she was beginning to feel. Why did Stephen have to act this way on their last night together? All summer he'd been so great, such fun to be around. And now, just when they should be saying a nice good-bye, he was behaving like a jerk—acting as if they were Romeo and Juliet! Yet, somehow she couldn't bring herself to leave. Not knowing what else to do, she whispered, "Stephen, please . . . I don't want to talk about this. I just want to say good-bye."

For a long moment he stared at her, his eyes glittering in the darkness. "All right, Janie," he said quietly. There was another pause, then suddenly his voice was fierce. "I'm going to go now. But for God's sake, at least send me away with a kiss."

"What?" She took a step backward.

All at once he moved through the darkness that separated them. Seizing her by the shoulders, he pulled her close. She was too taken aback to protest. And then his lips were on hers. They burned into her like a desperate brand. Janie had always thought of Stephen as a kid—but there was nothing childish in his kiss. These were the arms of a strong and passionate man, not a boy. She could feel the wildfire emotion that was coursing through him. With a will of its own, her body started to melt into his—her lips softened; her heart began to pound. An unfamiliar heat spread through her veins—she'd never felt like this with Ward! Her fingers touched his waist, feeling the strength of him. Suddenly she knew she was on the edge of discovering him as she never had before.

"Oh, Janie, Janie," he whispered. His hands were on her hips, pressing her close to him. Janie felt his powerful arousal. All at once, shocked and frightened by the intensity of his emotions—and her own tingling reaction—she tore herself away. One of his hands, tangled in her hair, caught at the fine chain around her neck and it snapped. But she ignored it.

"Good-bye, Stephen," she cried out, and then, giving him no chance to answer, she dashed across the street to the safety of her residence hall. But once inside, she leaned against the door shivering. *I'll never see him again,* she thought. And she was overwhelmed by a haunting feeling of loss.

CHAPTER ONE

It was nearly ten years since Jane had last been on Skyler's campus, but now she was back. And as she approached Killingworth Hall she took a deep, satisfying breath. The new semester was under way and autumn in Vermont promised to be beautiful. The sky sparkled like a sapphire canopy, the air was crisp with promise, and all around rich glints of gold and scarlet laced the velvety green of the trees.

Around her, students filled the walkways. "How'd your summer go?" a redheaded youth demanded of a pretty blonde in a fuzzy pink pullover.

"Super!" the girl responded, grinning.

Sharing their exuberance, Jane grinned too. She'd been nervous when the day had started, wondering whether she would measure up to this new career. But now that she'd met her first three classes, and they hadn't been so scary after all, she was more relaxed. The high spirits of the students all around were contagious.

Suddenly her own first days as a student here didn't seem so very long ago. What's more, as a youth passing by on a bicycle gave her a flirtatious wink, she was conscious that she still didn't look much older than these young college girls.

The thought dampened her buoyant mood slightly. A neatly put together blue-eyed blonde with a sprinkling of freckles across her uptilted nose, she had from her early teens been cursed with an Alice in Wonderland appearance. "Baby-face," her ex-husband, Ward, had sometimes called her. And after their first few months of marriage, it hadn't been a term of endearment. In the last few years, though, she'd lost a bit of weight, and her face had taken on a less girlish cast. Her cheekbones were clearly defined, and her blue eyes were no longer naive. With her thick, silvery hair twisted into a sophisticated knot on top of her head, she hoped she was finally beginning to look the part of a mature, capable woman.

Shifting her grip on her heavy briefcase, Jane picked up her step. Now that she'd successfully managed to get through those first three classes, the only thing left on her schedule was a faculty meeting in Killingworth Hall's auditorium. After delivering her first music lit. lecture to over three hundred students, she'd been tired and tempted to skip the meeting. But its purpose was to introduce new faculty members, and Jane was determined to start her new career on the right foot.

When she found a seat toward the back of the auditorium, it was already nearly filled with professors, instructors, and teaching assistants. Just as she'd suspected, a few minutes later the dean of arts and sciences gave his introductory greeting and then began calling out names of additions to the teaching staff. Jane was the first asked to stand.

"Ms. Jane Cowle, our new choral instructor, has joined us after receiving her degree from Northwestern. We look forward to many fine performances from her and her students."

Smiling, Jane acknowledged the brief applause and sat down, thankful she'd chosen a seat at the back. From her vantage point at the rear of the auditorium, she had an excellent view of the other newcomers being presented.

One by one, several instructors and a scattering of assistant and full professors stood up. They all looked so confident and dignified. Would she be socializing with any of them in the future? she wondered. She'd learned that when you were a single woman not particularly interested in dating, it could be awkward to make friends in a new place. Wives distrusted you, and unattached men didn't know what to make of you.

At that moment she was startled from her musings by a name that, when it was announced, jumped out at her.

"And now," the presiding administrator boomed, his monotonous voice suddenly enlivened, "I am pleased to present the notable young composer Stephen Hammond. He's come all the way from Hollywood to join us this year, and we are honored to have him on our campus. We've all enjoyed his music in such spectacular films as *Star Flights* and *Space Unlimited.* But this year promises an even more stellar event for our university community." The speaker paused to heighten the drama. "Mr. Hammond will be staging his first opera in conjunction with Skyler's music department later this semester. So we can look forward soon to our own gala premiere."

Jane's fine eyebrows shot up. She rarely went to the movies and had never been to either of those films. But the name Stephen Hammond was very familiar. Stephen, a big-name Hollywood composer? It had never occurred to her to make the connection. And then she got another shock. Toward the front, Jane's eyes suddenly picked out a head of thick, curly dark hair and a pair of broad shoulders. The shoulders, in their well-worn corduroy jacket, leaned forward lazily and the trim, muscular, jean-clad body below them rose. There was applause and a rippling murmur of interest. Then the dark head turned slowly toward the back and Jane took in the aquiline face and deep brown eyes that belonged to it. She inhaled sharply.

My God, it *was* Stephen! In this crowd of staid and balding professors that head of luxuriant raven locks stood out like a peacock spreading its tail in a barnyard full of geese. For a moment Jane's mind reeled. Since she'd come back to this small, distinguished New England campus last week, the past had been nostalgically reconstructing itself in her mind. But now it jumped out at her like a Jack-in-the-box yelling "Surprise!" Stephen Hammond, the friend she remembered from that long-ago summer when she was a junior at Skyler, had been a thin young man with an air of coltish eagerness. The confident, authoritative set of this man's tall, broad-shouldered body was completely at odds with that memory.

Would he see and recognize her? Jane wondered. It was very unlikely. Still, as his dark gaze moved to the back of the auditorium, her mouth began to curve up in a smile. But the smile died. Stephen's gaze swept past with no sign of recognition. Unaccountably, she felt hurt. Which was ridiculous, she scolded herself. The room was full of people and she was at the back. Stephen had no way of knowing she would be there. Though she *had* been introduced, it had been under her married name. If he hadn't turned around when she stood up, he would have no reason to connect Jane Cowle with the Janie Maclett he'd known. And even if he *had* turned, maybe she'd changed more than she realized. After all, they'd been friends just that one summer.

As it so happened, Stephen *had* spotted the delicate blonde in the back row. But he'd long ago trained himself not to stare at women with those particular looks of hers. Turning forward again, he resumed his seat and prepared himself to endure the rest of the introductions and the president's closing remarks.

For the next thirty minutes Jane sat in a state of suspended animation, staring in perplexity at the dark head in front of her. When all the new faculty had finally been introduced, a speaker made a few more comments which sailed past her unheard. Then the hour was at an end.

Following some polite applause, the audience got up to leave. Low-pitched murmurs were punctuated by laughter as professors and instructors streamed slowly up the aisles. But Jane remained in her seat. Her gaze was riveted on Stephen's tall form. As he started to stroll lazily toward the doors, the man behind tapped him on the shoulder and engaged him in conversation. Affably, Stephen bent his head to speak to the shorter man, and Jane watched in fascination. Was there any chance he might see her and stop to say hello? she wondered.

But as he passed her seat his eyes remained fixed on his companion. He did not pause or look in her direction. To hide her stab of disappointment, Jane bent to pick up her briefcase. It couldn't be that he was snubbing her. The Stephen she remembered had been a terrible tease, but unfailingly kind and considerate.

She stepped out into the almost empty aisle and began to make her way toward the door. Outside, however, she paused again, shifting her briefcase unconsciously from one hand to the other as she once again spotted Stephen. He was standing not more than twenty yards away, finishing his chat with the man who'd accompanied him from the auditorium.

For a moment Jane wondered what to do. A wave of shyness swept through her as she remembered how they'd parted all those years ago. She had a dim recollection of Stephen getting drunk and trying to kiss her. What if he didn't want to be reminded of old friendships? But that was ridiculous! He probably didn't even recall what had happened that last night at the end of the summer semester. And they were going to be working in the same department, after all.

Taking her briefcase firmly in one hand, she began to move in his direction. As warm memories of their camaraderie flitted through her mind, she stood waiting for him to finish his conversation and notice her.

While she bided her time she took advantage of her chance to study him. In the unseasonably warm, late-afternoon sun, he'd taken off his jacket and slung it over one shoulder. His sartorial habits hadn't changed much, she reflected. She couldn't remember ever seeing him in anything but jeans and a sweatshirt in the old days. Yet the snug denims clinging to his lean hips and the casual oxford-cloth shirt he wore now affected her quite differently than they would have ten years ago—perhaps because the body beneath them was no longer that of a lanky youth but of a mature, confidently masculine man.

At that moment the professor with whom Stephen was conversing waved a cheerful good-bye and turned to go. Jane cleared her throat. Stephen's dark head swiveled and his eyes narrowed. Looking up into his lean, deeply tanned face, it was easier to see the boy he had been in the man he was now. But though the eyes and mouth were much the same, there was none of the unsettled look that she remembered.

This Stephen's features were chiseled and diamond-hard. Though there was still that spark of wayward amusement lurking at the corners of his lips, he looked both experienced and tough. And there was a sexuality radiating from him that she didn't remember at all. But, of course, he'd been living and working in the film industry all these years. A successful man with his looks could probably have his pick of beautiful women.

Glad that he couldn't read her mind, Jane said pleasantly, "There's no reason why you should remember, but I think we've met. Did you spend a summer here years ago?"

There was a long pause. He took his time surveying her, his face still, not altering its expression by a breath. Then he folded his arms over his broad chest. "Yes," he replied calmly, his voice deeper and more resonant than she remembered. "You're Janie Maclett, aren't you?"

Stephen felt as if he'd been poleaxed. So the blonde in the back row he'd been ignoring because she looked like Janie was in fact really Janie. His mind seemed to go into overdrive as he sought to cope with this stunning turn of events. The girl who'd starred in so many of his youthful fantasies was now standing before him, lovelier than ever and smiling as if nothing more were between them than a cup of tea and some idle gossip about the weather. Of course, as far as she was concerned, that was true.

When Stephen said her name Jane relaxed a bit, and once more a smile began to bloom on her soft mouth. So he did remember her. "Jane Cowle," she corrected him. "I was married."

"Yes," he agreed evenly. "I recall you had a boyfriend by that name. So you married him?"

Something in Stephen's tone made Jane's gaze drop away. Though there had been nothing hostile about the question, she found herself remembering that he hadn't liked Ward.

"Yes," she replied, searching for a graceful way to make her getaway. There suddenly seemed no reason to continue the conversation. Though he was being polite, Stephen Hammond wasn't exactly overwhelming her with enthusiastic overtures of friendship.

"Your husband was a lawyer. Does he practice here in town?"

Jane shook her head. "No. Ward and I were divorced several years ago."

Stephen's expression darkened but he made no comment. She waited for the embarrassed "Oh" that was the customary response. But there was nothing. And suddenly Jane was anxious to retreat.

"It was nice seeing you again," she said politely. "I expect we'll be bumping into each other now and then in the music department. But if you'll excuse me, I have to get home."

He nodded, but as she started to hurry away she knew his gaze was on her back. Her mind swirled with confusion. Then she heard her name called.

"Jane, wait!"

Astonished, she turned to see him hurrying toward her.

"Do you really have to go?" he asked. And then, taking a deep breath and cradling his jacket in the crook of his arm, "Look, it's been a long time. We have a lot of catching up to do. Why don't you let me buy you a cup of coffee at Blake's?" he offered, naming a cafe that had been a favorite with them.

An automatic refusal hovered on Jane's lips. She was miffed that he'd been so cool before, as though he had no intention of renewing the acquaintance. But he was looking at her now with a concerned expression in his dark eyes. And suddenly he no longer seemed so much the haughty stranger, but more like the friend she remembered.

"Okay," she finally agreed. "Coffee sounds good. I haven't been back to Blake's yet," she added. "It will seem like old times."

"Sure, old times," Stephen murmured, directing her to the walkway that led to South College, where most of the bookstores and campus shops were lined up in a row. For a moment she caught that disturbing ironic coolness in his voice again. But when she shot him a questioning look he only smiled back, his white teeth dazzling against the deep tan of his face. Then he demanded in a bad Humphrey Bogart imitation, "What's a nice girl like you doing in a place like this, sweetheart?"

Jane grinned up at him, her eyes beginning to sparkle. "I'm a low-paid but respectable instructor," she informed him a bit self-consciously. "How do you like that? Remember how you yelled at me when I told you I was going to give up singing to marry Ward? Well, after all these years, I finally have a graduate degree and I'm going to teach choral music."

"With a voice like yours you shouldn't be teaching, you should be performing," he answered gruffly. "And yes, I remember our arguments—every word, every syllable, every flash of your big china-doll eyes, every angry sniff of your haughty little nose." He shook his head. "How long have you been in town?"

"Only a week. How about you?"

"Less than that, actually. But I've been lucky. I was able to lease a house from a biologist on sabbatical. It's completely furnished, so all I had to do was walk in and dump my suitcase full of dirty laundry on the floor and I felt right at home. The best part is that the place is on Lake Dunmore and hidden by trees. Now that the tourist season is ended, I have all the privacy I want. I've been so busy exploring the area that I haven't gotten into town much until today."

Jane nodded. That was probably why they hadn't run into each other before. She had once visited the area he'd spoken of. It was a beautiful gem of a lake surrounded by wooded mountain slopes—a great spot to swim and water-ski. And the hiking was good too. She knew of a mountain trail nearby that led up to a tiny lake on top of a low peak. But an isolated house on Lake Dunmore would be lonely in winter, she judged.

"Have you become a recluse?"

"No, but I've learned to enjoy my privacy. And since I spend so much time composing cacophonous music on a synthesizer, privacy is almost a necessity. Remember how you used to call my stuff a lot of 'weird noise.' "

Jane laughed. She had to admit she'd turned up her nose at Stephen's peculiar-sounding compositions. She'd teased him about his electronic music, and he'd teased her back about still living in the last century.

"How about you?" Stephen was saying. "Where are you living?"

While he carried on this conventionally polite conversation, Stephen's thoughts rushed down a different track altogether. Ever since coming back to this place, his mind had been on the past. Now it was walking beside him, divorced, apparently available, and more wrenchingly beautiful than ever. The question was—what should he do about it?

"I've been lucky too," Jane responded to his question. "I found an apartment right away. It's a darling little place over a carriage house within walking distance of campus. It used to belong to Carlie Black, the music department's secretary. You've probably met her?" She lifted her eyebrows inquiringly and Stephen nodded.

"Yes, cute dark-haired little thing who definitely likes to talk. This morning when I stopped by her desk for my schedule, she cross-examined me for twenty minutes. I was tempted to stuff a sock into her mouth."

Jane couldn't help laughing. "That's Carlie all right. Though I've only been in town five days, I feel all settled in. The afternoon I moved into the apartment she stopped by from work with David, her little boy. And she's been doing it ever since. It's like having a ready-made family."

"Not a bad thing when you're new in town," Stephen commented, pausing in front of a store window to inspect a colorful display of books.

"No," Jane agreed. "But I don't think it's really me she's visiting. It's the apartment. Before her divorce she lived there with her husband. Afterward she decided to move back into the big house at the head of the drive with her folks so she could get the extra income from renting."

As she spoke Jane was suddenly aware of her image reflected next to Stephen's in the store window. They made an attractive couple. Her delicate fairness seemed the perfect foil for his tall, roguish darkness. She cocked her head. His curls were as uncontrolled as ever, so why did the glossy black halo framing his lean features strike her as sexy whereas before it had always seemed merely messy? Arrested, she couldn't stop herself from staring at the picture they created together.

Just then Stephen glanced up and met her gaze in the mirrorlike glass. His eyes hadn't changed either. They were still dark and beautiful, fringed with the longest lashes Jane had ever seen. Quickly she looked away, feeling her neck go hot. It was absurd to think of Stephen as anything but a friend. That was how she'd always seen him—just a friend.

To mask her confusion, she began hurrying toward Blake's, half a block away. Stephen fell into place next to her, but he said nothing. The silence between them stretched until they reached the charming but rather dingy ancient campus hangout.

Ushering Jane in, Stephen commented dryly, "So you and your landlady are both divorcées struggling to make ends meet?"

As she led the way toward a painted wooden booth, Jane nodded. She didn't like the way he'd put it, but it was certainly true. There had been an instant bond between Carlie and her. Only a divorced woman could really understand another, she mused wryly.

"Funny," Stephen drawled, looking down at her with a hooded gaze as she slid in behind the table, "I would have guessed that alimony payments from a lawyer like your ex-husband would have left you pretty comfortably fixed."

Jane stiffened. It was unlike Stephen to be so rude. "When Ward and I were divorced we had no children, and I didn't ask for a lot of money," she told him curtly. "What I got I've spent on my education."

"Have you been in school ever since the divorce?"

Jane shook her head. "No. I knocked around New York for a year, trying to make it as a singer. I did some commercials and nightclub spots. But I finally concluded that show business wasn't on my dance card and decided to go back to school."

The harsh lines of Stephen's face softened. He rested his wide shoulders against the high back of the wood booth, regarding her steadily. "New York is tough. Even with talent like yours, it can take years to break in. You shouldn't have given up so soon."

"I'm not a kid anymore. I haven't got time to hang around hoping for my big break."

Stephen's gaze was pinned on her face. "I have some contacts in Hollywood and New York. There are people I could introduce you to if you're game to give it another try."

Jane was surprised and touched by the unexpected offer, but she shook her head firmly. "Thanks. That's sweet of you. But the truth is I'm not cut out to be that sort of performer—auditioning for parts, never being sure of anything. It's time I built something solid."

Stephen wondered why her marriage had failed if it was stability she longed for. Why did she need to start building "something solid" at this stage in her life? And why, once a man had a woman like Janie in his life, would he let her go? Surely even an uptight prig like Ward Cowle would have more sense than that. But instead of saying what was on his mind, Stephen asked, "Are you hoping to do that here at Skyler?"

Jane shrugged. "I'd rather hear about you," she told him truthfully. "Ten years ago you were a crazy young guy with impossible ideas. Now you're a big-time Hollywood composer. How did it happen?"

His dark face split in a wide grin and suddenly he was the old impish Stephen. "It was simple, really. Dumb luck. Let me go get us each a cup of coffee and then I'll describe my perilous climb to tinsel-town notoriety. You like yours with double cream, right?"

Jane was astonished. "After all these years you remember how I take my coffee?"

"Oh yes," he told her as he rose lazily from the booth. He let his warm, dark eyes move over her slowly. "I remember everything about you, sweet Jane."

CHAPTER TWO

A few minutes later Stephen returned bearing a tray weighted down with buttered bagels and two thick crockery mugs of aromatic coffee.

It was peculiar to find a cafe in a small Vermont college town that specialized in bagels. But Blake's were the best, and the sight and smell of them brought back memories. "Oh, Stephen," Jane murmured, "I used to dream about sinking my teeth into those. Do you remember how we came here and gorged ourselves after that canoe trip?"

He nodded and set her plate and mug down on the table in front of her.

As she recalled the tranquil beauty of that excursion, Jane's smile faded and she cast him a wistful glance. She didn't suppose there was much chance he would take her canoeing again, though the early autumn weather would be perfect for it. He might, for all she knew, even be married.

The thought impelled her gaze to his hands, which were curled around the warmth of his coffee cup. The long brown fingers were bare. It shocked Jane to realize how relieved she was not to find a wedding ring on them.

"You promised to tell me about your career," she said brightly.

He slanted her a look of amusement. "I've been

lucky there, I guess." Stephen revolved his white mug slowly on the napkin. "You remember how I was always writing stuff that I never got around to finishing?"

She nodded. He had perpetually been in the throes of some impressive project that he would lose interest in a week later when he got some new, even more impossible idea.

"Well, when I left here at the end of that summer and went back to California, I got serious. I finished my education and worked like hell."

Ruefully, he shook his head and took a sip of coffee. "I must have a closet full of completed compositions from that period of my life. One of my teachers had a contact at Colossus Filmways. When the studio started production on *Space Unlimited* and went on the lookout for theme music that was different, he recommended me." Putting his cup down, Stephen winked at her. "My music was the strangest-sounding thing they could find on short notice. As a result, I've been composing for the movies ever since."

Jane gazed at him. "That wasn't luck, that was talent. To get where you are now, you had to impress a lot of people."

"Success is mostly a matter of being in the right place at the right time."

"You make it sound so simple."

"It has been." His expression was reflective. "Maybe too easy."

"I have to admit," Jane commented, "it's a surprise to find you, of all people, writing for the movies. I never pictured you in Hollywood."

He looked at her curiously. "Does that mean you thought of me now and then over the years?"

"You popped into my head from time to time,"

she conceded with a smile. "But I imagined you starving in some garret in Greenwich Village or San Francisco, not squiring around Hollywood lovelies and driving a pink Cadillac."

He laughed. "I drive a red Maserati that breaks down every ten miles. I also own a rusted-out Volkswagen bug. Since my Maserati spends most of its time in the repair shop, the bug is my usual transportation."

"What do your Hollywood friends think of your split personality?"

Stephen shrugged. "People in never-never land tend to be tolerant of weirdness."

Jane laughed. "A good thing, in your case."

"I always did like to go my own way," he agreed good-naturedly. "That hasn't changed. In fact, ornery cuss that I am, starvation in a garret is probably what I deserve. Maybe that's why I took a sabbatical to do *Caitlin* and now another six months off to see it produced—even though there's no chance it will ever have any commercial success. I felt, as an artist, I needed to pay my dues."

Jane guessed that he was referring to the opera that had been mentioned at the faculty orientation. "Do you think it's a new direction for you?"

Stephen shrugged. "*Caitlin* is my pet project. But I don't see myself going on indefinitely composing operas no one cares to hear. I want my work to have an audience. I'm still interested in earning a living."

He must earn considerably more than just a living, Jane reflected. In fact, his income must be astronomical. How strange life was. For Stephen, who'd never seemed to care about money or success, both had fallen into his lap like ripe fruit. While she, who'd desperately wanted security and stability, had found neither.

During the next half hour they chatted amiably. Stephen had always been easy to talk to, but now he was a polished raconteur, amusing her with hilarious stories about life in Hollywood. He also asked her about the courses she was teaching, and she, in turn, queried him about his opera.

As they exchanged polite conversation, Stephen found himself wondering again what he should do. There was no question that he was feeling the way he always had about her—like a starving mutt confronted with a juicy bone. The years hadn't changed that a whit. Given his undeniable attraction to the woman across from him, the logical thing was to ask her for dinner, reestablish their old friendship, and perhaps from there move on to something more. It might not be so impossible. After all, he wasn't the bumbling youngster he'd been ten years back—nor was she the wide-eyed innocent. Yet, he hesitated.

In truth, his feelings for the Janie Maclett he remembered from a decade earlier were so complicated that he wasn't sure how much was real and how much just an impressionable young boy's adolescent myth. He did know that somewhere along the line she'd become a nostalgic golden memory, an emblem of his youth and his first lost love. Maybe it was smarter not to disturb ghosts from the past. Maybe it was better just to leave them locked in their shrines.

Once more Stephen began to slowly rotate his cup between his palms, and Jane was suddenly very aware of his fingers—long, deft, sensitive—the hands of a musician. Oddly enough, she had never noticed his hands during their earlier friendship.

Glancing up at him, Jane caught the intense look in his brown eyes as he stared at her. And suddenly she felt uneasy. She'd eaten her bagel and her coffee was cold. Glancing at her watch, she exclaimed, "Oh dear, it's time for me to get going."

"Why? Do you have an appointment?"

"No, but it's getting dark earlier these days, and I have to walk home."

"There's no need for that. I leased a small station wagon. It's parked near here. I can give you a ride."

She shook her head firmly. "No, I need the exercise. Besides, it's beautiful out this time of year. I'll enjoy the walk."

Stephen's dark eyes remained fixed on her. Then, as if he'd made a decision and wasn't entirely happy with it, he sighed. "All right," he said. "It was great to see you again, Jane."

"It was wonderful seeing you and talking about old times."

He smiled politely. "We'll have to do it again."

"Yes, we will," she agreed. "Soon."

Yet, when Jane walked out of Blake's she had the feeling that they wouldn't be meeting again. During the next couple of weeks it turned out that she was right. She saw Stephen in the office from time to time. And now and then she caught glimpses of him pacing across campus with his long-legged stride. But though he was as charming as ever when they ran into each other, his flashing smile was no warmer for her than it was for everyone else, and there were no further invitations for coffee.

Part of her was disappointed and rather hurt. Other than Carlie Black, she hadn't met many people on Skyler's campus, and it would have been nice to have a friend. But part of her was just as glad. Jane was honest enough to admit that she was not reacting to Stephen in the way she had when they'd been younger. It was unsettling to be around a man who attracted her. She didn't need that right now.

Making a success of her job and building a new life—those were the important things.

Yet, she couldn't escape him entirely. For one thing, Carlie loved to gossip and Stephen Hammond was one of her favorite subjects. The two young women had become friendly, and occasionally Carlie asked Jane to baby-sit her young son, Davy. Jane always agreed, for she had quickly fallen in love with the youngster.

One Saturday in October, Davy crouched in a corner of Jane's apartment playing with a set of blocks while the two women chatted idly at the kitchen table.

"The trouble with a guy like Stephen Hammond is he's too darn eligible," Carlie complained as she gathered up her jacket and purse. Carlie always seemed to be on the run, darting about like a waterbug and talking nonstop all the while. She was the opposite of her quiet son.

Jane lifted an eyebrow questioningly. "Too eligible?"

Carlie started to walk toward the door. "With those gypsy looks of his, he's got so many coeds drooling over him, I doubt if he even bothers to glance at females over twenty-one." She sighed wearily. "Which certainly cuts me out."

Jane laughed at her. "Come on!"

"No, really," Carlie insisted. "Haven't you noticed how the music department is suddenly swamped with nubile sophomores? Professor Hunt says we haven't had so many girls declaring themselves music majors in decades. And now that Hammond is getting ready to cast his opera, would-be sopranos are squirming out of the woodwork."

Jane shrugged her shoulders. Even though Carlie was exaggerating, what she said had a grain of truth. Jane had seen the pretty young girls who gathered around Stephen's office door in chattering thickets. Some of them were her students, so she'd heard rumors of the excitement building over his opera. It was an innovative and original work, she'd been told, and its production would do a lot to enhance the department's prestige. Under different circumstances, Jane would have been eager to audition for it herself. But something about Stephen's behavior made her hesitate. If he'd wanted her in his production, wouldn't he have said something?

"I really appreciate your taking care of Davy for me," Carlie said as she walked out onto Jane's small porch. "I hate to leave him on the weekends, but I really have to do some shopping."

Jane followed her, leaning against the door. "I enjoy having him."

Carlie squinted into the dazzling October sun and hurried down the steep flight of steps to her car. When she had backed down the long, narrow drive, Jane went back into the living room. She smiled down at Davy. He had arranged the colored blocks into an intricate pyramid and was trying to balance the last piece on top. It teetered and then tumbled, taking half the pyramid with it. Davy stared at it mutinously, his face going red with frustration. But when Jane knelt to help him rebuild the structure, his good humor was restored.

After the pyramid was finished she sat back on her heels and grinned at him. "What would you like to do now?"

David looked up from the blocks with a hopeful expression. "Bake a cake."

Jane chuckled and then ruffled his mop of straight brown hair. "I might have guessed. Well, I knew you were coming, so I bought the ingredients yesterday." She got up, took his small hand, and led him toward the kitchen.

What would it be like, she mused, if David were her little boy? Shortly after her first year of marriage to Ward, Jane had become pregnant. But that pregnancy had terminated in a miscarriage. She had been bitterly disappointed at the time, imagining somehow that a baby might make things right between them. Afterward, Ward had insisted that she protect herself against another pregnancy. Now she was glad. A child would not have saved their marriage. But sometimes, when she saw an appealing youngster like David, she ached with an unfulfilled longing.

The baking took up the next hour and was a huge success as far as Davy was concerned. It delighted him to lick the mixing bowl and nibble on the chocolate icing. But when he'd downed a large, moist slice of cake along with a glass of milk, he began to show signs of restlessness. Small wonder, Jane thought, peering through the window at the golden autumn afternoon which beckoned outside. It was much too gorgeous to spend the rest of the day indoors.

"How about a walk to the park?" Jane suggested as she cleared away the last remnants of Davy's snack. The little boy agreed excitedly, and after Jane found his jacket and pulled on a light Windbreaker for herself, the twosome were out the door and on their way.

As she strolled along the tree-lined street Jane was very glad she'd made the suggestion. It was another piercingly beautiful fall day. The sky was a rich blue studded with small, fluffy white clouds. The trees were splendid now in their full autumn regalia, their brilliant scarlet and gold tints making a breathtaking contrast against the rich azure sky above. She hadn't bothered to tie back her hair, and it hung in a silvery swath down her back. Unconsciously, Jane smiled. She enjoyed the sense of well-being that the beauty of the day and Davy's trustful hand in hers imparted.

When they approached the entrance to the park Jane looked down at the youngster. "Would you like to go to the river and watch the boats?"

He nodded enthusiastically, and they headed onto the path that led to the water. Jane had strolled there by herself several times in the past few weeks. It was another place that called up memories. The stretch of river fronting the park's boathouse was where she and Stephen had gone canoeing years earlier. *It seems a lifetime ago,* Jane thought as she looked down at the smooth, green water flowing gently past the weathered dock. Canoes in shades of stained blue and gray lay bottom-up on the concrete apron facing the pier. She smiled and waved at Davy, who was skipping between the boats exclaiming over their sizes and shapes.

"Can we go for a boat ride?" he pleaded, calling up to her.

Jane shook her head regretfully. "Not today. I didn't bring enough money with me. Maybe next weekend, if the weather is nice and your mom says it's okay."

Davy's round face clouded, but he made no more protest. Jane observed him with sympathy. She didn't know a lot about children, but she suspected that Davy was an unusually accepting youngster for his age. Was it because he was unsure of himself? she mused. And might that have something to do with the breakup of his family?

She, too, had always been unsure of herself. She had been too uncertain to protest when, immediately after their brief honeymoon, Ward had taken her back to his luxurious family home in Boston and installed her in quarters on the top floor of their elegant, rambling mansion.

"You'll be more comfortable here than in the cheap little apartment we'd be able to afford on our own," he had explained. "And while I'm starting out in the firm I'll be too busy to be home with you much anyway. You and Mother can keep each other company."

His prediction had turned out to be more than accurate. Ward had been completely preoccupied with building his career. On the rare occasions when he did make it home in the evening, he was much too exhausted, he informed her, to carry on conversations or go out. All he wanted after dinner was to fall into bed and sleep like the dead so he could be fresh for his next marathon day.

But it wasn't just overwork that made him so eager to sleep, Jane suspected bitterly. After he'd gotten out of school his intense ambition seemed to change him. Lovemaking between them, never a great success, became less and less satisfactory. Though she tried to respond, Ward's abrupt demands left Jane cold. After a while he seemed to lose interest, and weeks would go by without his even touching his young wife. There must be something wrong with me, Jane had told herself miserably, without having any idea how to fix it.

And then there were the parties. Jane felt like a failure in bed, but she knew she was even more of a flop at the endless round of socializing Ward demanded of her.

"It's vital to my career that you be a good hostess

and that we be seen at the right places with the right people," he insisted. But Jane was not a good hostess. When they asked Ward's boss to dinner she inevitably produced a disaster in the kitchen. And among the elite Bostonians with whom Ward wanted to rub shoulders, she was intensely uncomfortable and frequently tongue-tied.

"I can't believe the dumb things you were saying to the Harrises!" Ward once exploded. "Talking about the weather, as if it weren't the most boring conversational topic in the world! They must think I married a moron. And sometimes that's what I think too!"

Shivering at the memory, Jane pushed her hands deep into the pockets of her jeans and turned to gaze out over the bright surface of the water. A canoe was gliding softly into shore. A pretty girl with auburn hair perched on its prow. Laughing with her as he paddled was a lean, dark man wearing a frayed gray sweatshirt. On its front was emblazoned a large picture of Minnie Mouse. The man was Stephen, and as he stood up to jump out of the shallow vessel and onto the dock, Jane stiffened.

He was the last person she wanted to meet now, and her eyes darted around, futilely trying to find somewhere to hide where she would not be seen. But that was impossible. So she gamely stood her ground, listening with an odd, hollow feeling to the lighthearted banter between Stephen and his pretty companion.

Gallantly, Stephen helped the redhead alight. While he restored the life preservers to the boatkeeper, the girl flung herself down on a bench to rest. As she stretched and yawned, her curvaceous figure, in tight cords and a knitted turtleneck, was displayed to full advantage. Carlie is right, Jane thought. She hasn't got a chance. Why should Stephen look at her when he has girls as young and pretty as this at his beck and call?

It was several minutes later when Stephen finally noticed Jane. He turned to climb up the grassy knoll where she stood just above the boats. All this time she had been watching him, taking in the healthy gleam of his dusky locks, the broad shoulders beneath the outrageous sweatshirt, the narrow hips in close-fitting jeans.

Why had she never felt the impact of his attraction all those years ago when they'd been friends? It seemed so blatant now. Had he changed so much in the intervening years? Or was she seeing him differently because she'd changed?

He turned just at that moment, and their gazes collided. His thick brows lifted. "Hello there. I didn't see you."

"No, I know you didn't." She gestured lightly at the river and the boat. "Lovely day for canoeing."

But as her eyes surveyed the idyllic scene they suddenly flew wide with alarm, and the polite words she'd been about to add froze on her tongue. In her preoccupation she'd forgotten about Davy. He'd ventured out onto the boat dock and was teetering on the edge now as he leaned far over to peer down into the water.

"Davy," she cried, her voice vibrating with alarm. But as she started to run down the small hill, it was already too late. The sound of her cry seemed to knock the youngster off balance. In the next instant he toppled over into the river and floundered there helplessly. Jane had just reached the dock when Stephen raced past her.

"I'll get him," he flung over his shoulder. Throwing himself down on the weathered planks, he levered over the edge so that his long arms touched the water. In the next split second he had grasped Davy's shoulders and hauled the thrashing child back onto the dock like a wet fish.

Davy landed in a pool of water, howling with fear while Jane looked on in distress.

"Hey, it's okay, you're all right now," Stephen assured the child, brushing his sopping hair out of his eyes. "But I think we'd better get those wet things off you."

His words jolted Jane into action. "Yes, I can give him my jacket," she offered breathlessly. She dropped to her knees and hurriedly unbuttoned Davy's sopping shirt. When his jeans and wet underwear had been stripped off, she started to unzip her Windbreaker. But before she could take her jacket off, a muscular brown arm stopped her.

"Here, put this on him," he ordered, handing her his sweatshirt. "Good old Minnie to the rescue."

Startled, her head swiveled around and she gazed up at Stephen. Above the snug waistband of his jeans, he was naked. His broad chest was deeply tanned, and it took Jane's breath away. Hurriedly she turned and pulled the warm sweatshirt over Davy's damp hair.

It looked absurd on him, of course. The waistband hung down to his ankles, and the sleeves were twice as long as his short arms. But it would keep him warm. Still, what was Stephen going to do? There was a crisp chill in the air, and he couldn't spend very long walking around with nothing on.

When she turned to him he was no longer on the dock. He was talking with the girl who'd been in his canoe. Jane watched them together, wondering if the attractive redhead was someone special in Stephen's life. It certainly hadn't taken *him* long to make friends on campus. Ducking her head, Jane turned back toward Davy.

A moment later Stephen rejoined them. She half expected him to be irritated. This incident couldn't have added to his afternoon. But he looked his usual good-humored self, his deep brown eyes sparkling as if he and his lady friend had just shared a joke.

"If you and Esther Williams here are ready, I'll drive you home," he said, playfully tousling Davy's hair.

"But your friend," she began to object, looking where the girl still stood smiling.

Stephen brushed away Jane's protest. "Joanne says she was ready to call it a day, anyhow. One more hour with the world's worst canoeist and she would have been the one to throw herself overboard." He turned to aim a playful salute at the redhead which she returned jauntily. "She's got her own car, and she has a tennis match this afternoon. Let's go home."

Except for Davy's periodic complaints, the ride back was accomplished mostly in silence. Stephen asked a few polite questions but seemed preoccupied. After giving him directions, Jane settled into the station wagon, holding a damp and subdued Davy in her lap. She was acutely aware of the man next to her. His wide, naked shoulders filled the seat so that she shrank back, afraid of brushing against him.

When the car pulled into the long drive leading to her apartment, Jane removed the sweatshirt from Davy, who was almost asleep, and replaced it with her own Windbreaker.

"There's no need," Stephen told her, accepting

the garment with a distracted frown. "I'll pick up something to wear at home."

But Jane was anxious to avoid the further embarrassment of having to return his clothing. "Davy will be all right in my jacket until we get inside." She pointed up at her apartment. "Thanks for your help," she added, shooting him a polite smile.

Stephen stopped her. "I'll carry him up."

Before she could argue the point he was out of the car, tugging Minnie down over his head as he strode briskly around to her side. In swift movements he opened the door and hoisted Davy into his arms.

"We'll have you inside and warmed up in a jiffy," he assured the little boy. Then, while Jane followed anxiously behind, he climbed the steep flight of stairs with sure, steady steps.

The moment they were indoors Jane took Davy from Stephen's arms. Her mind was concentrated now on making sure the child did not take a chill. Quickly she thanked their rescuer again, and then, not pausing to see him out, hustled Davy into the bedroom, where she tucked him in under the blankets for his afternoon nap.

"I'll go and get you some dry clothes," she told him after he'd snuggled happily under her warm quilt.

But to her surprise, when she went back out into the living room Stephen was still there. He was standing with his back to her, glancing idly through some of her books. She stopped at the door and stared, conscious of the sudden breathless feeling in her chest. Why was he waiting around?

Hearing her uncertain step, he swiveled and looked her up and down. "Your apartment is very nice, but don't you find it cramped for raising a child? I imagine a boy your son's age takes up a fair amount of space."

Jane's forehead creased in a faint frown. "David isn't mine. He's Carlie's son. I think I mentioned him to you earlier."

Stephen nodded. "Oh yes. Now that I think of it, you did say that you and Ward had no children when you decided to divorce."

"That's right."

"How long were you married before you decided to split?"

"Five years." Her eyes strayed to the door, but Stephen didn't take the hint.

"Then you've been on your own now for almost another five years?" He paused, then added, "Carlie tells me that you never date. I wonder why. You were a lovely girl, and now you're a beautiful woman." He paused again. "I have no business asking you this, Jane, but I'd really like to know. Are you still hung up on your ex-husband?"

She stared at him. Her mouth was dry, and she couldn't think how to answer. "No," she finally managed.

Stephen took a step closer and looked down at her through his lashes. "Do you remember that night ten years ago when we saw each other for the last time? I got drunk and behaved like a fool. You laughed at me, and when I tried to kiss you goodbye you ran away."

Jane's blue eyes widened, and she felt color begin to creep up her cheeks. So he hadn't forgotten.

Stephen's eyes continued to dwell on her flushed face. "Jane, I've been thinking about that night lately, thinking that I'd like a second chance at it."

With slow deliberation and with the confidence of a man who was accustomed to having his way with women, his hand reached out and curled around her chin. Then he leaned forward to brush her lips with his. A part of her sensed at once that the light, impersonal kiss was all he intended, and she waited in a kind of suspended animation to be released. But the touch of her mouth on his seemed to ignite a reaction in Stephen that he hadn't anticipated. Briefly she felt him struggle against it. Then he succumbed. Hauling her close to his body, he plundered her lips as if she were treasure that had once been his and which he now intended to reclaim. Still too startled to react, Jane stood like a statue in his arms.

One of Stephen's hands anchored itself in her loosened hair, immobilizing her head. He drew back for a moment and sighed roughly as he looked down into her wide, surprised eyes. And then, with another sigh, he closed his eyes and kissed her again. Only this time the sensuous caress was an appeal. His free hand stroked the back of her neck and then traveled down her spine and curved possessively around her hip, molding her slender body to the taut contours of his. While his hands held her to him, his mouth explored hers tenderly.

Jane began to feel a slow fire kindle somewhere deep inside of her. It was such a poignantly beautiful feeling that she was tempted to let it grow. But then a scene from the past knifed through her mind, shredding the fragile web of her response.

"A man needs a real woman," Ward had told her the day he'd packed his things and moved out. "I can talk to Annette as an equal, and behind closed doors she makes me feel like a king. You're a nice kid, Janie, but you're no damn good in bed."

The cruel memory banished her feelings of pleasure. Suppressing the shiver that had begun to chill her skin, she remained tensely still in the circle of Stephen's arms, her hands not moving and her body stiff and unyielding.

He loosened his grip and then reluctantly stepped back. "I'm sorry. I didn't realize I was going to do that."

"I know you didn't. It's all right. It doesn't matter." She didn't meet his eyes.

He ran an impatient hand through his curls. "It isn't all right. And it does matter. Jane, will you let me take you out to dinner? We have a lot to talk about."

Still not looking directly at him, she shook her head. "No."

Before she'd been hurt because he'd seemed not to want to renew the friendship. But after that kiss she knew friendship was no longer the issue. Attractive though she found this man, she simply wasn't prepared for what he was offering.

" 'No' you can't, or 'no' you won't?" he asked quietly.

Finally she lifted her face and he found himself looking down into wide blue eyes so troubled that they made him flinch.

"Stephen, let's just forget this."

For several painful heartbeats he continued to watch her. Then he turned away. "All right," he said as he reached out to open the door. "If that's the way you want it. We'll forget all about this."

CHAPTER THREE

During the next couple of weeks, when Jane and Stephen ran into each other on campus or in the office, he seemed no different than he had been before. Though his dark eyes lingered on her thoughtfully, his smile and his ready laugh appeared as unshadowed as ever.

Irrationally, the fact irritated her. She didn't know why it should. She didn't want to join what was probably by now a long line of conquests, did she? But Jane knew that really wasn't the issue. When he'd kissed her in her apartment it wasn't that she hadn't wanted to respond. She had wanted to—very much. It was simply that she'd been afraid.

Stephen had always been an effortless charmer. True to form, by the time the semester was a few weeks old, he'd developed a following of devoted students and a wide circle of friends. As Jane strolled across campus one afternoon late in October, she spotted him stretched out very much at his ease on the grass. He was holding a guitar, strumming idly on it from time to time as he chatted with the group of adoring students sitting all around him. Most, though not all, were girls. Several Jane recognized from her own class in choral music.

Her blue gaze picked out a head of frizzy red hair and she smiled. The flaming topknot belonged to

Alberta Gundersen, a tall contralto given to punk hairdos and purple toenail polish. The girl had real talent. Jane had made her one of the soloists in the Christmas production of *The Messiah* that she was coaching. Alberta was now gazing at Stephen as if he were the pot of gold at the end of the rainbow. Just then, however, she looked up. Leaping to her very substantial feet, she began to wave wildly. "Oh, Ms. Cowle, Ms. Cowle!"

Jane hadn't wanted to be noticed and cursed her luck. Doing her best to look unruffled, she strolled over to the group.

Though it was very late in the month and piles of leaves lay at the foot of trees in gold and scarlet mounds, the weather was warm. Almost no one was wearing a jacket. Stephen had on a blue work shirt open at his throat so that a dusting of black chest hair was just visible. Below the shirt his hips were encased in the inevitable snug-fitting jeans. On his feet he wore sneakers that were probably very comfortable but were so scuffed and ragged that they looked like candidates for a trash bin. As he watched Jane's approach he pushed back an unruly lock of raven hair and squinted into the sun. His lashes were so long that behind their thick screen Jane could only just barely make out the glint of his watchful dark eyes.

"Well, this is certainly a picturesque scene," she commented, striving for a light tone.

"It's fate that you came along just now," Alberta bubbled in her throaty voice. "We've been talking about folk music. Mr. Hammond says that no one but Joan Baez has been able to perform 'The House of the Rising Sun' the way it was meant to be sung because no one else has had a soprano pure enough and strong enough for it. But I said I'd heard you sing snatches of stuff in class and I thought you'd be able to do it just as well."

While Alberta beamed happily, Jane's jaw dropped. "Well . . . thank you," she stammered. "That's quite a compliment. But, really, I . . . I . . ."

Suddenly, Stephen, who'd been lying on the grass studying her, rose to his feet and, with a grin that was pure mischief, offered his guitar. "Be a good sport, Ms. Cowle, and settle this dispute right now," he drawled. "Give us your version of the song."

Jane stared at him with widening eyes. She was not amused. She glanced around at the grassy area criss-crossed by cement walkways leading to all the buildings on campus. It was dotted with students and faculty either sitting in small clusters on the grounds to enjoy the fine weather or meandering to and from classes along the paths. "You want me to sing 'The House of the Rising Sun' here, now?"

"Sure, why not?"

She met his ingenuous gaze and then watched one of his level black eyebrows slowly lift. Her shoulders stiffened. He must be aware that she knew the song. In the old days they'd sat on the stoop of his rooming house and sung it together. Was he wondering if she could still hit those high notes? Well, she could. She hadn't spent the last five years training her voice, making it strong and flexible, for nothing. Indeed, she knew that she was a much more self-assured performer now than she'd been as an undergraduate.

Accepting his challenge, she set down her books, took the guitar from his hands, and ran her slim fingers experimentally over the strings. After tightening two of them, she strummed the opening chords and then began the hauntingly beautiful folk song.

Propped on his elbows, Stephen lay on the grass listening to Janie's crystalline soprano. Ten years ago it had been lovely. It was even more so now. Since she was completely caught up in the ballad, he could study her at his leisure. She was certainly doing the song justice. Not only did she sing like an angel, she had the face of one too. He tilted his head, watching her lips as they formed the bitter-sweet words. He'd have to possess no imagination at all not to remember how they'd felt against his. He'd given that kiss a lot of thought over the past couple of weeks—not only because of Janie's puzzling reaction, but because of his as well.

There was no point in kidding himself any longer. Though he'd met most of the eligible women on campus and taken out quite a few of them, they were all just substitutes for the real thing. He wanted Janie. Even though she'd been about as responsive as a wooden figurehead when he'd made a pass, nothing was changed. And trying to pretend that wasn't true only made it worse. Maybe there was only one way to exorcise the silver-blonde with the big blue eyes. His expression grew thoughtful. He'd have to give that some consideration.

After finishing the last verse Jane was disoriented for a second or two. That always happened when she performed. No matter what, no matter where, she became completely wrapped up in the music. She was almost startled by the burst of applause from the small audience of students.

"That was great!" Alberta exclaimed heartily. "I knew you'd do it just as well as Joan Baez!"

Several others chimed in with compliments. But

while Jane acknowledged all of these graciously, she was most curious to hear what Stephen had to say and turned to look at him expectantly.

With all the panache of an eighteenth-century swashbuckler, he leapt to his feet and bowed deeply from his waist. Then he reclaimed his guitar and smiled directly into Jane's eyes. "You haven't lost your touch. I never got more pleasure from hearing that song than I did just now."

"Thank you." She wished she had a better reply. But she was feeling a little dazed by the adrenaline pumping through her system. She avoided the compelling sparkle of his gaze, nodding and smiling and trying to look everywhere but directly at him. Then she glanced at her watch. "Thanks for the kind words. I needed that! But I'm already late for a lecture I was planning to catch."

"Can't you stay and give us another song?" Stephen asked. He strummed a chord. "I'll be your accompanist."

But Jane shook her head, and over the friendly protests of the students, she waved and then turned away. As she hurried along the brick pathway she asked herself why she hadn't stayed. True, she *had* been going to a lecture. But it certainly wasn't anything she couldn't miss. It would have been fun to sit on the grass with those kids, singing songs while Stephen played the guitar. She had an introverted nature, and it had always been hard for her to feel comfortable with new people. But Stephen would have smoothed the way and made it easy—just as he had all those years back. Why hadn't she let him do it?

But Jane knew why. It was because of that disturbing kiss. There was no hope that she and Stephen could ever be just friends again. *A good thing he's going back to Hollywood at the end of the school year,* she told herself.

Jane hadn't had anything like the almost instantaneous popularity Stephen had achieved on campus, but she was beginning to make friends. There were several other female instructors her age whom she was getting to know, and through Carlie's good offices she joined a bridge group that met every other week.

"It was fun," Jane acknowledged as she and Carlie walked home from the first meeting. "But the gossip was flying pretty thick and fast over those cards. Since I don't know everyone on campus yet, I found it hard to keep up."

Carlie chuckled sympathetically. "Most people around here are pretty nice, but Skyler is a small place. Since there really isn't much else to do for entertainment besides gossip, everybody knows everybody else's business." She paused. "When I was getting my divorce I felt as if I were doing it in a goldfish bowl."

"That must have been tough."

"It was. Sometimes I think that instead of divorcing, we should have just tried settling somewhere else and starting fresh. Everyone knew what he'd done, so even though he asked me if we couldn't put it behind us, I said no. There was no chance for a new start here. And, of course," she added, "I was so angry that I wouldn't listen to anything he said."

Jane looked at her new friend sideways. Though Carlie talked about everyone else, she rarely mentioned her ex-husband. She had confided, however, that their marriage had broken up because he'd been unfaithful. Though Jane could certainly sympathize with Carlie's feelings, she couldn't think of anything to say that would help.

"Speaking of goldfish bowls," Carlie went on brightly, "didn't I see you having coffee with Dan Wilkens the other day?"

"Yes," Jane admitted. "He wanted to talk about the Christmas program."

Dan was a nice guy in his middle thirties who taught in the music department and he was a bachelor. But though he'd asked Jane out several times, she'd put him off. She was still unsure of how to handle that part of her social life in Skyler's rather inbred community. And though she liked Dan, she didn't feel the slightest attraction.

"Dan likes you," Carlie commented. "I can tell by the way he looks at you. Are you going to date him?"

"I don't know," Jane hedged.

Carlie shot her an assessing look. "Dan isn't the only one who looks at you as if you were a hot butterscotch sundae just waiting to be gobbled up. When you came into the office to pick up your mail yesterday, I saw Stephen Hammond watch you until you disappeared into the elevator. It wouldn't surprise me if you're the next one on his hit list."

"What do you mean, 'hit list'?"

"Well, he's certainly going through the women around here awfully fast. I don't think he's dated anyone more than twice. My guess is your turn is coming up soon, so prepare yourself."

"You're imagining things," Jane muttered, but she felt a shiver of anticipation at the thought.

There was a price to pay for the warm, golden October that everyone on Skyler's campus had enjoyed. When November came the sun disappeared behind a thick blanket of gray clouds as if it never planned to show its face again.

The first Friday of the month a cutting wind blew Jane into the office. Members of the music department convened for biweekly meetings on the last day of the work week. Before each of these get-togethers Professor Hunt, the department chairman, put a copy of the agenda in everyone's mailbox. While Jane unwound the wool scarf swathing her neck and head she picked her agenda out of her box and studied it. As she read down the short list her delicate eyebrows lifted. The main topic of discussion was going to be *Caitlin,* Stephen's opera.

Lately Jane had been hearing a lot of rumors about it from her students. A few of them, including Alberta, had auditioned for the production and received small roles. Word was, however, that the lead part hadn't yet been cast. Jane wondered if the problem would be raised at the meeting.

An hour later, when all the department members were gathered around a conference table, that was exactly what happened.

"Well, Hammond, if you're ready to present your report, I'll gladly turn the meeting over to you," Professor Hunt volunteered, smiling beneath his neatly trimmed gray mustache.

Stephen leaned his sinewy forearms on the table. He was wearing a navy-blue turtleneck sweater and had its long sleeves pushed up to his elbows. Jane couldn't help but think how wonderfully handsome he was.

"Except for one role," he announced, "my opera is cast and I'd like to get started with rehearsals as soon as possible. However . . ." He raked a hand through his thick locks. "The part left unfilled is crucial. It's the role of Caitlin herself."

"The lead is supposed to be a soprano, isn't she?" Dan asked.

When Stephen nodded Professor Hunt joked, "Well, last time I looked, we weren't short of those. In fact, of late they seem to be multiplying around here like fruit flies."

Though everyone else around the table chuckled, Stephen looked only mildly amused. "It's not that a lot of young ladies with high voices haven't made appointments to sing for me," he pointed out. "Take my word for it, I've listened to so many off-center high C's that I leave my studio reeling. The problem is that the lead role in my opera calls for a very special singer, one with an unusual range and flexibility and great purity of tone. The success of the thing really depends on that, and, unfortunately, I just haven't found her."

Jane looked down at her hands. She couldn't help thinking of herself and wondering if Caitlin were a part for which she would be suited. But it was not a question she was going to express aloud, not even if she had to bite her tongue.

At that point, much to her chagrin, Professor Hunt spoke up. "Has our Ms. Cowle auditioned for the role? I haven't heard her voice lately, but by all accounts, she sings like a canary." He gave Jane a broad smile.

Suddenly all eyes, including Stephen's, were on her, and she knew she was going to have to respond. She cleared her throat. "I've been very busy with my classes and with settling into a new place. Also I'm beginning rehearsals for the Christmas concert. It hadn't even occurred to me to audition for Mr. Hammond's opera. In fact, I didn't even realize that the auditions were open to faculty members."

"Oh, all campus productions are open to faculty," Professor Hunt quickly clarified. "In fact," he added, "I'm surprised Hammond hasn't asked you to try out before now." He looked back at Stephen, raising bushy inquiring eyebrows. "Didn't you know Jane was a fine soprano?"

The attention had now switched to the lean dark man across from the department chairman. Jane half expected that Stephen might look irritated at being pressured to consider her for his opera. She found it extremely embarrassing. Surely, if Stephen had wanted her to try for the part, he would have said so before now.

Yet, there was nothing in his expression to indicate anger or exasperation. Indeed, if she'd been looking closely enough, she might have seen a gleam of triumph in his deep brown eyes.

"I'm well aware that Jane Cowle has a fine voice," he drawled. "But Caitlin will be a difficult part to learn and a taxing one to perform. I had no reason to think she'd be willing to take on all the extra work. And," he added, "I was far too shy to ask."

Everyone laughed at that. Shyness was not part of Stephen Hammond's vocabulary.

"Well, Jane," Professor Hunt said when the merriment finally died down, "will you consider auditioning? If this performance is a critical success, it will add a great deal to the department's prestige."

Put like that, the request was impossible to refuse. "Why, why yes," she agreed. "Though perhaps it will turn out that the role will be more than I can handle too."

"That could be," Stephen agreed. "Can you come to room 213 in the music building tomorrow afternoon at four? We'll find out then."

"All right, I'll be there," Jane answered.

That evening she spent the hours after dinner on voice exercises—doing a very thorough job of running through scales that she normally tended to skimp. Jane was proud of her voice. From a very early age it had shown signs of being remarkable, and when she'd first gone to college her education had been financed partly from a scholarship she'd won in a talent contest. In a way, when she'd given up singing in order to marry, she had also given up part of her identity. After the breakup of her marriage, reclaiming that abandoned talent had meant a great deal to her. And during the years when she'd struggled to piece her life back together, what she took to be her one solid asset had assumed even more importance.

Stephen had already heard her sing a folk song. But the demands of an operatic role would be an altogether different sort of test. She was determined that when she auditioned she would turn in a creditable performance.

As the hands on her wristwatch crept toward four the next afternoon, and she walked down the corridor toward room 213, she was every bit as keyed up as she'd been trying out for Broadway shows a few years back. Which was silly, she told herself. It wasn't the same thing at all.

When she tapped on the open door and strolled into the room, her stomach felt as if it were being tickled with a feather duster. It settled down only slightly when she spotted Stephen. His back was to her and she noted that he was wearing navy blue again, only this time it was a short-sleeved T-shirt that displayed to advantage his well-developed shoulders, broad back, and narrow waist. He was standing by the piano talking to a girl with long, straight black hair. The pretty student was gazing at him worshipfully.

"You need to think about the use of percussion some more, Tina," he was saying. "Go home and take some time to look over your composition, and if you decide to rework it, I'll talk the problems over with you again."

The girl smiled up at him, and even from across the room it was obvious to Jane that her heart was in her big brown eyes. "Oh, thank you," Tina breathed. "Mr. Hammond, I mean Stephen, I just want to say that your coming to Skyler has been the most wonderful thing that's happened to me."

He chuckled. "Better even than charge cards and designer jeans? That is a compliment."

As they laughed together Jane cocked her head. As far as she knew, Stephen hadn't dated any students. Yet, obviously they were throwing themselves at his feet. Smiling dreamily, the girl left and Stephen turned around to greet Jane. Her gaze fixed itself on the front of his T-shirt. In large white letters it read, "Your Average Maniac."

"All ready for your audition?" he inquired pleasantly.

She looked up into his face. "I don't know. I've never sung for a maniac."

Grinning, he retorted, "Just be glad it doesn't say 'Sex Maniac.' "

"That would unnerve me completely," she agreed. Slowly she walked to the piano, where he stood waiting for her. "Something tells me Tina wouldn't have minded it though."

"Tina? You mean the little girl who was just here?" His smile widened and he wiggled his eyebrows. "Why, sweet Jane, that's the first time I've ever heard you say something catty. I didn't know you were capable of it."

"There's a lot you don't know about me."

True, Stephen thought. But that didn't mean he wasn't going to find out.

"Do all your female students ogle you as if you'd just ridden a chariot down from Mount Olympus?" Jane asked.

"Most," he agreed cheerfully. "But being adored isn't as much fun as you might think. In fact, it can be irritating as hell. The coeds on this campus are damned aggressive."

"Oh really? If all your other admirers are as pretty as Tina, they must be hard to push away when they try to climb in your window at night."

Stephen's dark eyes sparkled with unholy humor. "Not at all. I prefer older women. But you already knew that, didn't you?"

The blunt retort caught her off guard, and she felt the back of her neck get warm.

"Now," he continued, "if you were to try scaling my drainpipe, I'd throw every sash in my house open and greet you with champagne and roses."

"I'm not the athletic type," she said more brusquely than she really intended. His flirting was making her nervous. She didn't remember his ever talking to her quite this way when they were undergraduates. But then, Stephen was no kid now. "Are you going to show me the music you'd like me to sing?"

He turned back to the piano and began to sort through a stack of scores. "Actually," he said over his shoulder, "before I give you something to interpret, I'd like to talk to you about the part."

With several sheets of music in his hand, he turned back and motioned her to sit down. After she'd settled into one of the student desks, he dragged the piano stool around and straddled it, facing her.

As she waited for him to speak Jane felt ridiculously self-conscious. She'd dressed very carefully for this audition and was wearing a camel-wool skirt that swirled mid-calf over soft leather boots and a coordinating thigh-length houndstooth jacket that she'd gone out and bought yesterday afternoon. She knew that she looked attractive and professional in the casually fashionable outfit. If anyone in this room deserved to feel uncomfortable, it should be Stephen. He was the one wearing a ridiculous T-shirt and jeans. Yet, as he lounged before her, he appeared utterly at ease. It was she who felt her nerves prickling at the surface of her skin.

Stephen had stopped his teasing and was now all business. "The part of Caitlin is very special. If you're to interpret my music correctly, it's important that you understand the character."

Unconsciously, Jane licked her lips. "Is my appearance okay for her?" she asked. Slightly built and of average height, she didn't have the commanding presence that so many operatic roles called for.

Stephen's gaze flicked over her face and figure. "Your looks are ideal."

Oddly that disturbed her almost as much as if he'd said she wasn't right for the part. "What sort of girl is Caitlin?"

"She's the embodiment of a dream, a walking fantasy."

Jane's eyes widened. "Do you mean that she's a ghost?"

"In a sense." Stephen leaned forward. Beneath his raven curls his eyes were intent, searching. "There's a theory that every man carries around with him the image of his first love." He paused, his gaze never leaving hers. "She's the girl he ached for but never had the courage to approach, and because she was always unattainable, she haunts his dreams for the rest of his life. Often even after he's made a commitment to another woman. To Jim, the hero of my opera, Caitlin is that girl. For him she represents the fantasy of idealized love." Stephen's gaze hadn't wavered. "That's why the role is so demanding and why the woman who sings it has to project just the right image."

His words had a very odd effect on Jane. Her eyes fell from his, and suddenly she felt flustered and almost afraid. "It sounds as if this Caitlin is supposed to be a sort of goddess. I'm not sure that I—or my voice—can live up to that."

"Oh, you can do it all right" he said with conviction. "I've never doubted that. It's just a question of whether or not you can get through the music. It's pretty demanding."

As he spoke he rose to his feet and withdrew a score from the top of the pile resting on the piano. Handing it to Jane, he said, "How about seeing what you can do with this? I'll give you fifteen minutes to study it. Feel free to use the piano if you like."

As Jane accepted the music her shoulders squared. Inexplicably, the moment Stephen had issued what sounded to her ears very much like a challenge, her nerves had settled down. She might not be able to project the image of an idealized love goddess, but if the music didn't require superhuman qualities as well, she was sure she could "get through" it.

Walking over to the window, she leaned against the wall and studied the notes on the page. She could see why the undergraduate sopranos on campus had flunked Stephen's test. It wasn't just a matter of range but of sudden fluctuations from middle C's to notes two octaves higher. That sort of attack required a great deal of control and confidence from a singer.

Unbuttoning her jacket, she took it off and draped it over a chair. Then she moved to the piano and began to run through the melodic line.

As she sat on the edge of the piano stool, her gaze fixed on the sheet of music, Stephen studied her. He'd strolled over to one of the student desks and ensconced himself. From his vantage point he had an unencumbered view of Janie's profile.

When he'd first seen her she'd seemed virtually unchanged to him. But since then he'd noticed that she'd altered a lot over the years. It wasn't just that she was slimmer, her delicate profile honed clean of the baby fat that had softened it when she'd been a teenager. The image she projected now was of a very self-contained young woman. In a lot of ways she'd been more of a child than he during their earlier friendship. She'd been less certain of herself, of what she wanted and who she was. And that, he supposed, accounted in part for her failed marriage. He wished he knew more about what had gone wrong, but she obviously wasn't going to say. And there was no way, in this decidedly fragile stage of their relationship, that he could ask.

His gaze lingered on her, taking in the clean line of her small nose, the shadow her golden lashes cast on her cheek, the soft fullness of her mouth. As her fingers ran over a particularly difficult set of phrases on the piano, she frowned. Her lower lip pouted slightly and Stephen found himself once more imagining its petal softness against his mouth. He'd kissed her only twice, and both of those encounters had been utter failures. What would it be like if she responded?

Slowly his eyes moved down the ivory column of her throat. She had her hair caught in a clasp at the back of her neck. Its pale gold sheen set off the deep rust of the sweater, which clung gently to her breasts. Though he'd repeatedly fantasized about Janie's breasts, he could only guess what they were like. Stephen shifted his weight on the hard chair. Well, before his stint at Skyler was over, the fantasizing would be at an end, he told himself.

She moved, startling him from his unsettling reverie. "I think I'm ready to give this a try now. Will you play for me?"

"Of course." He stood up, and when she'd taken a place next to the piano, he seated himself on the stool and readjusted its height. "Are you sure you're ready?"

"As ready as I can be without taking the music home with me to study for a night or two." That was really what she'd like to do, but she wasn't going to ask for any concessions.

His lids came down over his eyes, masking their expression. "All right then, let's begin."

He played the opening chords and then looked up at her expectantly. Her gaze was fixed on the music, but when the moment came for her to begin, her eyes, the color of periwinkle in spring, went to the beam of sunlight filtering through the dusty window. Her first tone was as pure as clear, cool water, and Stephen knew that he'd found his Caitlin. Only he'd never really lost her. She'd been with him all along. It had always been just a matter of time.

"You've got the role," he told her when she finished. "Rehearsals start next week."

CHAPTER FOUR

Wednesday afternoon, two weeks after her audition, Jane finally managed to tear herself away from her last group of students and head toward a four o'clock rehearsal for *Caitlin.* When she'd won the role she'd felt pleased and flattered. After she'd studied the whole score she'd been even more delighted. This opera of Stephen's was really exciting.

The part of Caitlin was particularly thrilling, and Jane felt grateful for the opportunity to take it on. Perhaps it was only going to be a college production, but Stephen was now an internationally known composer. Important New York critics would attend the opening. Even if that weren't the case, the music was the kind of thing almost any soprano would give her high C's to sing.

Nevertheless, as she pushed open the door of the rehearsal hall, she was feeling apprehensive rather than enthusiastic. Working closely with Stephen was turning out to be a strain. Indeed, the tension between them was now so thick that even the students were conscious of it.

"Whew, am I ever glad you're here!" Alberta greeted her in a stage whisper. Despite the frigid temperatures outside, the statuesque redheaded student was wearing a bright green leather miniskirt and sandals to match. "The boss is really in a bad mood. He's been stomping around for the last half hour wondering why you're always late."

"I'm not always late," Jane defended herself. "I do have classes to teach, you know."

"I know, I know!" Alberta moaned and rolled expressive green eyes. "Tell that to him. He's like a bear with a sore tooth today."

Jane looked toward the stage, where Stephen was talking to a young girl in the orchestra pit who was clutching a violin. You could always count on Alberta to be decked out in something outrageous, but with Stephen you never knew. Sometimes it was just work shirts and jeans. Other times it could be some casually elegant outfit. Today above denims he had on a scarlet sweatshirt that demanded in large white letters, "Beam me up, Scottie. There's no intelligent life down here."

When he wore T-shirts or sweatshirts with messages, they usually expressed his mood. She guessed he was not pleased with the way rehearsals were going. Jane had always thought of Stephen as casual and easygoing. But she was learning that was an image he unzipped and stepped out of when he was directing a rehearsal. Most of his cast might be college students, but he wasn't going to settle for any less from them than he would have asked of professional singers. With her he was even more exacting. Nothing but absolute perfection would do for his precious Caitlin. Stiffening her spine, Jane began to walk up the aisle.

When Stephen caught sight of her he stood up and scowled. Seeing Janie every day like this was maddening. On the several occasions when he'd casually asked if he could give her a ride home or buy her a cup of coffee, she'd turned him down. Because of his frustration, he was having more than his share of sleepless nights—which probably made him more irritable than necessary. But knowing that only shortened his temper further. "Well, well, so our star has finally arrived and we can begin," he drawled.

Ignoring the little jibe, Jane pointed at his sweatshirt. "That's an old one, you know. Trekkie stuff like that has been around for ages."

He glanced down at his chest. "Old, but apt. This rehearsal hasn't even started and already two members of the cast have informed me they've lost their music and the first violinist has resigned because of her math grades."

"Maybe that's just an excuse. Maybe she's backing out because you turn into the monster from the black lagoon whenever the violin section messes up one of your melodic lines."

"The premiere of this opera is going to be performed for an audience of adults, not indulgent parents who've come to hear their kindergartners recite nursery rhymes," Stephen shot back. "Like in the old adage, anyone who can't stand the heat should get out of the kitchen."

Before she could respond, he turned away and began shouting directions. Students scurried about the stage like the windblown leaves on the sidewalks outside the building. Sighing, Jane took several sheets of music out of her briefcase and stood ready to begin the farewell scene that set the tone for the rest of the opera.

An hour and a half later, feeling close to tears, she threw the music down on the floor, wrapped her arms around her chest like a shield, and glared at her tormentor. "I've sung this aria ten times and not once have you been satisfied. What in the world is it that you want?"

"I want the mood to be right, which means that you have to be projecting the correct emotion. What is it with you this afternoon? You've been singing with all the feeling of a Barbie doll!" But looking a lot softer and more touchable, Stephen thought, his gaze skimming over her longingly.

Jane's expression was mutinous. "I think you're being hypercritical."

He was about to snap back a retort when he suddenly became aware of the students who were standing about. Even if Janie refused to recognize what was really going on, they didn't. They all knew their esteemed director was short-tempered because he had the hots for his leading lady. Glancing around, he waved a dismissing hand. "All right, kids. Rehearsal's over. You can go on home for Thanksgiving vacation now. Remember not to OD on turkey. Be here Monday at four o'clock sharp."

There were a series of comments accompanied by groans and giggles. Then the other cast members shrugged into their coats and shuffled down the aisles. When the auditorium was finally emptied Stephen turned back to Jane. She was still standing in the same spot, her arms folded across her chest and her expression stony.

His tone became more conciliatory. "Janie, I'm not trying to be difficult. I'm just doing my damndest to put together the best possible production. Surely you don't fault me for that."

"Of course not." She unbent slightly. "I just think that in my case you're being unreasonable. This Caitlin character has assumed some kind of mythic quality to you. I wonder if anybody human can sing it to your liking."

"You can do it, you're just not trying hard enough."

"I'm doing my best."

"Then maybe you need some special tutoring."

"What?"

"I think you need to work intensively on the role and that I should coach you on a one-to-one basis," he told her softly. "How about coming to my house tomorrow morning and spending the day?"

"But tomorrow is Thanksgiving."

"I'm not doing anything special. Do you have something planned?"

"No." Carlie's parents had invited her to eat turkey with them, but she'd refused, not wanting to intrude on their family holiday. "I don't know . . ."

Stephen ignored her protest. "Then it's the perfect opportunity for us to do some real work together. Can you get to my place by ten?"

"I don't have a car."

"I'll pick you up."

She eyed him uncertainly. She really didn't want any personal involvement with Stephen. He was going back to California, so it had no where to go—and she had too much to lose. "Is this really necessary?"

"Absolutely. You may not have the same commitment to this opera that I do, but I think you'd like it to be a success. Isn't that right?"

Jane sighed. "Yes, yes of course I would." She still had her doubts about spending the day alone with him, but somehow she couldn't find the strength to put up a fight. They were just going to work together. Surely there would be no harm in that, she told herself.

At ten sharp the next morning Stephen's car appeared in her driveway. She'd been dressed and ready, waiting at the window watching for him. Before he could get out to come up and knock on her door, she was outside and running down the stairs. Stephen watched her hasty approach with an odd feeling in his chest. Like a general on the eve of an all-or-nothing campaign, he was feeling a bit nervous.

Fifteen minutes after she'd settled herself in the passenger seat, he guided the vehicle smoothly onto the winding road that circled Lake Dunmore. Surrounded by foothills, the small lake was an idyllic spot in winter. Even today, with the sky overcast and a damp chill in the air that threatened freezing rain or even snow, the area was still picturesque.

Jane was staring out at the choppy gray water when he swung the car into a short gravel drive. Before them stood a white clapboard bungalow with a huge natural stone chimney. Nestled among tall pines and oaks, the place had a homey look that she found instantly appealing.

"You must have a gorgeous view," she commented, eyeing the large windows which looked across the road and out on the lake.

"Yes," Stephen agreed. He slid out from the driver's seat and came around to open the door for her. "I like it."

Inside, the bungalow was even more welcoming. Oval rag rugs covered the wide, pine plank floors, which were scarred and mellowed with age. The overstuffed furniture was simple but comfortable, and there was a fire laid in the handsome fireplace. Jane was surprised by how clean and sparkling everything seemed. Somehow her host didn't strike her as the type to be a meticulous housekeeper. When she made a comment to that effect he shrugged and grinned.

"I had Mrs. McNeece come in yesterday to clean the place up."

After he'd taken her ski jacket and draped it, along with his parka, over the loaded clothes tree in the hall, Stephen knelt before the hearth and lit a match. Jane stood at the threshold watching as smoke began to curl up the chimney. In jeans and a cream-colored fisherman's knit sweater, he was dressed relatively conservatively today. The outfit suited him, she thought. But then so did silly T-shirts and old sweatpants. He was one of those rare men who radiated such total self-assurance that he would look appropriately dressed in a tuxedo or a Santa Claus suit.

She, on the other hand, had tried on and discarded several outfits before settling on gray wool slacks and a thick pullover patterned in pastel shades of blue, pink, and cream. Dragging her gaze from his broad back and narrow waist, she glanced around. There was an old upright piano next to the front windows. Its flat top was loaded with piles of music. Next to it stood a synthesizer. She surmised that Stephen must have had it shipped from California. Wandering over to the electronic instrument, she gazed down at the keyboard and its accompanying control panel. Remembering some of the wildly cacophonous music Stephen had composed as an undergraduate, she could just imagine the kinds of sounds he made on the synthesizer when he was alone here at night. Jane smiled. If any ducks out on that lake hadn't yet migrated, they must think a banshee had come to haunt the place. A moment later she was distracted by her host's cheerful voice.

"Well, that should do it," he said, rocking back on his heels. In the fireplace a bright, steady blaze had now flickered to life. "There's only one more thing for me to attend to before we get started."

"What's that?"

"I have to put the turkey in the oven."

Jane's eyebrows shot up. "You've got a turkey? I thought this was just going to be a work session."

"It is." Stephen strode out into the hall and back toward the kitchen. "But we have to eat something. So it might as well be a proper Thanksgiving dinner."

She started to follow behind. "Do you mean that you have all the fixings?"

"Just salad, baked potatoes, and a box of instant stuffing."

She hovered in the doorway, watching while he opened the refrigerator and took out a roasting pan in which reposed a modest-sized bird.

"Is there anything I can do to help?"

"Nope. It's pretty much ready to go. All I have to do is stick this in the oven and set the timer. An hour before it's supposed to be done, I'll put in some potatoes to bake."

"You seem to know your way around a kitchen," she commented as he adjusted the dials on the stove.

He glanced back at her over his shoulder, his expression faintly amused. "I've been a bachelor quite a few years now. I've had to learn how to feed myself."

The remark raised all kinds of questions in Jane's head. Surely he hadn't been by himself all those years. Surely, living in Hollywood, he must have had his share of female roommates. And why hadn't he married? Was he a playboy, a hardened bachelor? She had no idea. In most of the ways that counted, Stephen was a mystery man.

"Where do you live in California?" she asked. "Is it a place like this?"

"I have a house at the beach. But it's not a cozy little cottage. It's an A-frame with a terrific view of the ocean at sunrise." He slid the pan in the oven and then cast one last cursory glance around the counters before turning to escort Jane back to the living room.

"Do you get to see many of those sunrises?" Jane was quizzical. Somehow she didn't picture the man at her side as an early riser.

"More than my share," he replied. "But not because I jump out of bed at the crack of dawn. Usually it's because I've been up all night."

"Are you an insomniac?"

"In a way. I think that when I have something brewing in my head it must be a little like being in labor. I can't rest until the thing is born. I have to put the notes down on paper." When they reached the piano he turned toward her, an odd expression on his face. "Caitlin's realization aria was written during a spectacular sunrise. I'd been up all night struggling with the melody. When it finally came my studio was flooded with a glorious pink light that made the atmosphere around me seem almost incandescent." Why had he told her that? he asked himself. It was something he hadn't spoken of to anyone else.

She stared at him, suddenly able to picture the scene vividly. Stephen would be hunched over the piano, dressed in nothing but old cutoffs or pajama bottoms. His hair would be a wild tangle of black curls, and as the light reflecting off the ocean bathed him in a scarlet and gold wash, the expression on his face would be one of pure exaltation.

"I really can imagine," she said softly. "And the

aria deserves to have been born in a setting like that. It's one of the loveliest, most haunting things I've ever heard."

"Thanks." For a moment his expression was sober. Then he grinned in the old familiar way and said cheekily, "Correction, it's going to be the loveliest thing when you get it right. That's part of what I want to work on today."

While the turkey cooked, gradually filling the little house with its delicious aroma, they went over the music Stephen wanted to perfect. Though he'd occasionally been sharp with Jane at rehearsals, today he was the soul of patience. At times she considered him maddeningly picky; nevertheless, she also had to admit to herself that he was a good teacher. Where many musicians were incapable of expressing themselves except through their music, Stephen could put his concerns into words. Patiently, he tried to do that for Jane.

"Janie, when Caitlin rejects Jim, it's not because she's cruel or callous. That's the feeling you're projecting, but it's not right."

Jane looked at him. "Then why does she do it? He's just laid his heart at her feet, and she steps all over it."

Stephen smiled dryly. "She's young and naive. She's been so locked up in her own little fantasy world that she hasn't understood what's been going on around her. It's that innocent, well-meaning blindness of hers that you should be trying to convey." He looked at the clock on the wall behind the piano. "We've been working for three hours straight. It's about time for our turkey to come out of the oven. I don't know about you, but I'm getting hungry."

Jane nodded. Singing of the kind she'd been doing was hard physical labor that could burn as many calories as bricklaying or roadwork, and she was famished.

Back in the kitchen, Stephen moved around with efficiency, getting butter out of the refrigerator and popping rolls in the top of the oven to warm. When had he made the transformation from the gangly puppy she remembered to the strong, self-reliant man she saw before her now? Jane wondered.

"There must be something I can do to help. Would you like me to set the table?"

"It's already set, but you could get that bottle of Chablis out of the refrigerator and carry it to the dining room along with the salad," Stephen suggested as he took out the roasting pan and carefully set it on top of the stove.

"The turkey looks gorgeous."

"Not too bad for an inept bachelor production. Well, I'll just slide him onto a plate along with the baked potatoes and we'll be all ready."

The dining room, though small, was as charming as the rest of the house. They dined at a round oak table placed in front of windows overlooking the lake. In honor of the occasion, Stephen got out a lace tablecloth. The slightly chipped plates were an old-fashioned blue and white willow pattern and the silverware was an eclectic mix of stainless steel that had obviously seen a lot of service.

Maybe it was because she was charmed by the setting and the company, but Jane didn't know when she'd had a better Thanksgiving dinner. After she married, the stiffly formal Thanksgivings with Ward's parents had been nightmarish for her, and since her divorce, lonely holidays had become days to get past and forget as soon as possible. Suddenly

Jane was grateful to Stephen for making this one into something that she would recall with pleasure.

"Do you spend Thanksgiving with your parents when you're back home in California?" she asked on impulse.

"Sometimes I go back home. It's not always easy, though."

"Why not? Your parents must be terribly proud of you."

"They're proud that I'm a success, but they don't really know what to make of me otherwise. I'm sort of the ugly duckling in the Hammond brood. I have two older brothers who were football heroes in high school and are now happily married accountants with 2.4 children. My kind of life doesn't make a lot of sense to them." That was the understatement of the year, he thought. Whenever he went back home his hulking Mr. Clean-type siblings eyed him as if he'd just landed a space ship on their roof. The only thing they ever asked him about was how many starlets he'd laid.

Now that Stephen mentioned it, during their early friendship Jane could remember him talking about his brothers. At that time he'd described them as jocks who had nothing but scorn for their skinny kid brother's weird interest in music. Stephen was no longer skinny. In fact, she guessed that he was now probably as broad-shouldered and muscular as they. But his life-style would still strike them as peculiar. "Is that why you never married? Because you didn't want to be like your brothers?" she blurted.

Stephen regarded her over the rim of his wineglass. "No, that's not why. I'd like to have a wife and family."

She was embarrassed that she'd asked the question. This was really none of her business. But now that she'd started it, she couldn't think of any graceful way of changing the subject. "You just haven't met the right girl yet," she finally murmured.

When he swallowed his wine his smile was slow and dry. "That's a very simple way of saying something complicated, isn't it? But in my case I'm afraid it doesn't fit. My problem is that I did meet the right girl. She just didn't know that I was the right boy." He glanced at his watch. "I want to get in three or four hours more work this afternoon. But I think we have time for a piece of pumpkin pie. Want some?"

Silently Jane nodded and watched with troubled eyes as he took their plates out to the kitchen. What had he meant by that remark? she wondered. Was there some lost love in Stephen's life? Again, it was none of her business. But that didn't keep her from staring out the window at the lake while a feeling of bittersweet melancholy closed around her.

When Stephen came back he was carrying huge slices of pie topped by small mountains of whipped cream. He noticed her down mood and instantly teased her out of it. By the time the meal was over and they'd washed up, the easy camaraderie of the morning had been reestablished between them.

It lasted through the rest of the afternoon and past the turkey sandwiches they snacked on when they were finally ready to put the music away. "You were right," Jane admitted as she took the last nibble of her sandwich and washed it down with a glass of milk. "This was a very profitable way to spend the day. I really do feel much more comfortable with the part of Caitlin than I did before."

Stephen took the plate out of her hand and set it down on the table next to the couch. Instead of having their light supper in the dining room, he'd suggested they enjoy it out in the living room in front of the cheerful fire, which was now throwing long shadows around the room. "It was just a matter of feeling your way into the role," he told her. "You're going to be fine."

"Do you really think so? I'm still intimidated by this magical woman you've created. I'm not at all sure I can live up to her."

Smiling faintly, Stephen reached out and caught a long strand of pale gold hair that had become entangled in her collar. "You will," he said, weaving the silken threads through his fingers and thinking that her hair hadn't changed. It was the same mesmerizing web that had been his undoing ten years earlier. "You'll not only live up to her, you'll be her."

Jane shifted uneasily and the golden strands fell away from her host's hand. "It's getting late. I should probably be going now."

"Oh? Why?" His expression was bland, his dark eyes curious. "It's only seven-thirty. I have a very good bottle of cream sherry that I've been hoarding for a special occasion. Stay and have a glass with me in front of the fire. After that I'll see you home safe and sound."

It was a tempting invitation. The wind was howling around the house, rattling the shutters. The couch in front of his glowing fireplace, on the other hand, was cozily warm. It took more resolution than Jane possessed to shake off the pleasant drowsiness that had stolen over her. It was nice to be in this hideaway with Stephen, watching him as he prowled around the room, admiring the snug fit of his denims on his narrow hips and the way his white sweater stretched across his shoulders. When he came back carrying two wineglasses half filled with a dark amber sherry, she reached out lazily.

"Tell me something," he said as she took the glass from his fingers. "Earlier you were asking me how I usually spent my Thanksgivings. How about you? Do you normally go home for the holidays?"

"What home?" Jane rolled the faceted glass between her palms and absently studied the way the flames were reflected in its prisms. "I don't really have a home now."

Stephen's eyes narrowed. "Let me see. Back when we were students, I remember you telling me that your mother had just remarried. In fact, that was why you were in summer school, wasn't it?"

"Yes." Jane nodded. "Pierre, my mother's new husband, didn't particularly want to be saddled with an adolescent stepdaughter on his honeymoon. Not that I blame him."

"You're not on good terms with your stepfather?"

"I've only seen him twice, so it's hard to say. Since their marriage he and my mother have lived in the South of France." She sighed. "I haven't been particularly lucky in the father department. I never did know my real one. He was an artist who died when I was a baby. Looking back on it as an adult, I realize how tough that must have been on my mother and I sympathize. But all I remember from my childhood is that she was hardly ever there."

"You were raised by your grandmother, weren't you?"

"Pretty much. Mother was a fashion buyer for a big department store in Philadelphia. She spent most of her time traveling, often in Europe. That's where she met her second husband, and from all accounts they're deliriously happy, so I'm glad for her."

Stephen took a slow sip of sherry and considered the woman before him. "What about your grandmother?" he asked gently. "Do you still see her?"

"She died the year I went away to college."

Stretching out his long legs and leaning back against the couch cushions, he reflected on that. "Let me see if I can put this all together," he mused. "When we first met you were hell-bent to marry Ward Cowle."

That was true, Jane acknowledged to herself. At twenty she'd been like a mule in blinders, her gaze fixed on the myth of "happily ever after." All during her lonely, unconventional childhood she'd envied the normal family life of her friends. Ward, with his all-American-boy good looks and solid background had seemed to represent the things she'd always wanted—stability, comfort, security.

"At the time," Stephen was saying, "I thought it was crazy for you to give up your education and a promising career as a singer when you had so much talent. But now I think I understand. You'd lost the grandmother who raised you. Your mother was abandoning you for a new life. You must have felt cast adrift."

"Yes," Jane said. She took a sip of sherry and felt it slide down her throat like liquid silk. Her lids slipped down and she gazed at the fire with sleepy blue eyes. "When Ward asked me to marry him I felt as if he'd thrown me a life ring. I didn't find out until later that it was a lead weight."

CHAPTER FIVE

Startled, Stephen scrutinized Jane's profile. "That sounds awfully cynical. Earlier today you asked me about marriage. How about you? Do you hope to remarry?"

"No."

The negative was so unequivocal that he was even more surprised. " 'No,' you don't have any hopes? Or 'No,' you don't want to?"

"Both." Jane squirmed. How had the conversation gotten onto this track?

"You must know that the 'hope' part doesn't make sense," Stephen persisted. "You're even more attractive than you were as a teenager. There are half a dozen bachelors around campus who'd like to date you, only you always give them the cold shoulder."

She shot him a look. "How do you know? Have you been gossiping about me?"

"What an insult! Men don't gossip. They exchange information."

"You mean they make suggestive remarks and tell dirty stories," Jane teased.

"That too." He looked amused and then slipped into an exaggerated movie-cowboy drawl. "Pardon me, ma'am, but haven't you looked in a mirror lately? You're a mighty pretty little woman who's stirred up quite a bit of male interest around these hyar parts."

"I'm a very ordinary-looking blonde."

"Ordinary?" Stephen's accent became crisp. "My God, Jane, that long yellow hair of yours is enough to excite male hormones for miles around."

"I can't say I've noticed anything like that." She pictured hormones flying helter-skelter like dust clouds in a windstorm and laughed at the idea.

"Then you're blind. It's certainly always had that effect on me." This was the first time Stephen had ever said anything like that to her, and even though she'd known there was more in the undercurrents between them than an old friendship warranted, it was startling to hear the words spoken so baldly.

"You . . . you find me appealing?" She could have kicked herself when the question slipped past her unguarded lips. It sounded more like an adolescent plea than a query.

In the shadowy light, Stephen's eyes seemed to grow even darker than they were, and she could see tiny flames from the fire reflected in their glittering surface. "Of course I do," he said huskily. "I always have. Don't pretend you don't know it."

She had known, yet his admission worked a kind of alchemy. All day she'd been sharply aware of Stephen, his voice, his body, the vital aura that permeated the ambiance he carried with him. But now, like a blue sky deepening to purple at twilight, that awareness intensified.

As her azure gaze locked with his dark one, she registered afresh every detail of his appearance—the glossy thickness of his curls, the way his brows grew in an almost straight line above his beautiful deep-set eyes. How could she have thought herself in love with Ward when she had this man with which to compare him?

When he took her glass and set it down, she didn't say a word. Once more he reached out to touch her hair, and she was unable to draw back. For a long time now, ever since that kiss in her apartment, she'd been struggling with a desire for Stephen's touch. Now, as she felt his long fingers gently comb through her tresses, she wanted to sigh with pleasure. Surely it would be all right to sit here quietly without protest just for a little while, she told herself.

"I think you must have the most beautiful hair in the world," Stephen said, his husky baritone reverberating in his chest. To him she appeared as lovely and desirable in the flesh as any romantic dream. He touched a finger to one of the tendrils that had sprung out to gild her temple and noticed the tiny pulse throbbing there. Could his touch be having on her anything like the effect she always had on him?

When she didn't pull away he grew bolder. Reaching down, he unclasped the tortoiseshell barrette that held her hair back against her neck. As the skein of thick, pale gold fell free, framing her face and tumbling loose around her shoulders, he was a lost man. Groaning, he leaned forward.

"Jane, what is it about you that moves me so? I wish to God I understood it."

She had no time to answer or even to consider what he meant. As gentle as the touch of a feather, his lips brushed against hers. The faint hint of sherry that lingered on his mouth blended with that on hers and she was captivated. If the kiss had been aggressive, she might have drawn back. But there was no coercion. The caress was hesitant, undemanding, and strangely bittersweet.

It was only a matter of seconds before Stephen drew away. For a long moment he studied her solemnly. "That was for old time's sake."

"Old time's sake?"

"Yes." His smile was crooked. "You don't know what the hell I'm talking about, do you? It doesn't matter. I don't want to talk anyway." Firmly, and with no hesitation now, he gathered her into his arms.

Jane did nothing to resist. What was happening seemed so right. Her body leaned into his warmth and her arms went to his shoulders, feeling the hard bone and muscle beneath the thick wool sweater he wore. This time his kiss held more real authority. Against her soft lips, his mouth was hard, as though in search of something and very determined to have it.

"Oh, Stephen," she gasped when his mouth at last abandoned hers. "This isn't a good idea."

"It's a great idea," he retorted huskily. With sensuous delicacy, his lips began to move along the curve of her cheek. Her eyelids fluttered closed as he dropped a tender caress on each, and then with the tip of his tongue carefully traced the feathery gold of her long lashes. "Just relax, Janie," he whispered. "There's only good here. You know I would never hurt you. I only want to hold you and kiss you."

It was so tempting to believe him. Outside, the wind howled, but here next to the fire, cradled in this man's strong embrace, she did feel safe. The sherry she'd drunk was warming her blood, but it was no more intoxicating than the feel of Stephen's mouth caressing her skin. In his arms her body felt almost unfamiliar, as if it belonged to some new, freshly created being. All her senses were alive, and she was both languorous and electrically awake, her nerve centers excitedly registering unfamiliar sensations while her limbs grew strangely heavy.

Jane's hand moved up from Stephen's shoulder to test the texture of his hair. She shivered as his mouth found her ear. Taking the lobe between his teeth, he nipped gently. The playful gesture made her smile and rub her cheek against his. The low-pitched growl of pleasure he made deep in his throat worked on her senses like an aphrodisiac. With her eyes closed, she pictured the way his black curls must look against the pale gold of her own long, straight locks. The image entranced her.

Tipping her jaw back, she sighed as he dropped a line of kisses along its sensitive underside. Somewhere in the back of her mind she knew this was a mistake and that she must put a stop to it. But the message wasn't getting through to the rest of her body. Or, rather, the rest of her body was refusing to receive it.

For Stephen it was like a dream. The firelight, Janie's hair freed and spilling around her throat and shoulders so that he could breathe its perfume, feel its silken caress against his cheek. It was like revisiting a fantasy. Only suddenly life had magically been breathed into what had seemed a hopeless phantasm and it had been made flesh.

Janie's pliant body fit perfectly in his arms, just the way he'd always known it would. Her skin, glowing in the flickering light from the fireplace, was like warm satin. Reverently, he dropped a slow kiss into the hollow of her throat. He could feel the throb of her heart against the beating in his own chest. Was this really happening at last?

As if to test the reality of the moment, his hand slipped beneath the hem of her sweater. She stirred slightly when she felt his fingers against the bare flesh of her rib cage. But his mouth went back to hers and he set about kissing her into acquiescence. As his mouth made love to hers, moving from side to side, tasting, exploring, Jane's resistance faded and he sensed with a fierce burst of triumph that some of the passion he was struggling to leash in himself was now beginning to strain in her.

When her lips finally parted, allowing him to deepen the kiss, he felt his pulses leap. As his tongue grew bold and ransacked the sweetness of her mouth, he lowered her back against the couch cushions. His hand still lay against her rib cage absorbing the delicacy of its structure, the silky smoothness of her skin. But it wasn't enough. He wanted to touch her breasts. He'd been wanting that for ten years, and now that the opportunity finally presented itself, there was no way he could restrain the desire.

As Stephen's tongue tangled with Jane's his fingers found the soft mounds they longed for. Through the thin fabric of her bra his thumb rhythmically circled her breasts' tips. To his immense satisfaction, they stiffened in response and he felt her gasp against his mouth, but still she didn't try to push him away.

Jane's thought processes seemed to have abandoned her entirely. All she could do was feel, and what she was feeling was so pleasurable that she couldn't make herself want it to stop. The Stephen who held her in his arms now was very different from the awkward boy who'd once forced himself on her. With just a few simple kisses he'd awakened a hunger that had been sleeping in her for a long time. This was a man who knew about women and who was employing all his considerable expertise.

As if by magic, she felt that her sweater was no longer covering her ribs. The snap on her bra loosened and then the garment was gently pushed aside. Stephen's mouth closed around the glowing tip of her naked breast and she inhaled sharply at the exquisite pleasure. As his tongue swirled about the desire-hardened bud, all Jane could do was arch back and sink into a warm sea of sensation. She wasn't even aware that one of his hands had gone to the waistband of her slacks. But when she felt his fingers on her stomach, she began to surface from her euphoria.

Then his hand slipped smoothly beneath her panties, and she jerked into an abrupt consciousness. All at once she was painfully aware of herself, of her surroundings. Stretched flat on the couch, her body was all but covered by Stephen's. He'd pushed her sweater up and unzipped her slacks so that her breasts and belly were exposed.

Her fingers closed around his wrist, stilling the disturbing explorations of his hand. "No, Stephen! Please stop!"

Instantly he went rigid. Rearing his head, his dark gaze flew to hers. As she looked up into his face she saw the excitement glittering in his eyes, the hard flush along his cheekbones, the tightness around his mouth.

"Don't stop me now, Jane."

"Yes, yes I have to. I'm sorry." And she was sorry—miserably so. How had she let this happen? Self-consciously, she tried to tug her sweater down. Stephen's warm, hard palm still lay flat against the quivering flesh of her bare stomach, and he showed no sign of moving away.

"Tell me what's wrong, Janie. You wanted this—maybe not as much as I do, but you wanted it."

There was no way she could deny the truth. It was all too obvious. "Yes." Her gaze slid from his, but as he continued to look down into her face, she knew what he was seeing. Her cheeks were aflame and her lips were still swollen from the kisses she'd accepted so willingly seconds earlier.

"Then tell me what's wrong. It's not as if we don't know each other. We've known each other for years."

Struggling, she managed to sit up. With obvious reluctance, Stephen took his hand away and she was able to tidy her clothes and zip up her slacks. All the while, she could feel him watching her. What was he thinking? That she was a tease, a prude? Did he imagine she'd deliberately led him on?

"We don't really know each other," she said, still not looking at him. "I'm a different person than I was ten years ago, and so are you."

"The years make superficial changes. But underneath we stay the same."

"Not me. I'm different."

Stephen's eyes narrowed. "Tell me how. I want to understand you."

She shot him a quick look. He was sitting back against the couch cushions, regarding her intently. Once again she looked away and stared into the fire, not really seeing it. "When you knew me I was an inexperienced kid. Now I'm thirty years old, a woman who's survived a failed marriage and who's rebuilding her life. I can't let anything ruin that."

Stephen was silent for a moment, digesting this. "I think it's time you told me about your divorce."

"No."

"Tell me, Jane. You're hiding a lot beneath that

cool, controlled surface of yours, and you need to talk."

Again she glanced at him sideways. Usually there was laughter lurking somewhere in Stephen's expression. But now his face was utterly sober, his expression searching. She couldn't doubt his sincerity, and she felt as if she did owe him some sort of explanation.

"There's nothing much to tell," she said, taking a deep breath. "Ward walked out on me. He left me for another woman."

Stephen's gaze didn't waver. "That's tough. When it happened did it come as a surprise?"

"No. I expected it. In fact, I expected it to happen much sooner."

"Why was that?"

Jane cast him another look. Maybe it was the strong emotions she'd just experienced. Or maybe it was this time and place, isolated by the circle of firelight with the wind rattling the shutters outside. Or maybe it was just something about Stephen and the feeling of trust he evoked in her. She found herself want to confide in him. All the things that had been troubling her for years suddenly seemed to press against gates that were no longer sturdy enough to contain them.

Abruptly they came spilling out. "I was a complete failure as a wife, that's why."

Stephen's eyes widened. "A complete failure? What in the world makes you say that? In what way?"

"In every way. I wasn't a very good cook. I was a poor hostess, I was shy and tongue-tied at parties . . ."

"Those kinds of things aren't important . . ."

Stephen started to interject, but she ignored him and doggedly blurted out the rest.

"And I was lousy in bed."

There was a long silence. While it stretched around her Jane stared into the fire and listened to it crackle and pop as if someone had thrown tiny bullets into its flames.

When Stephen finally replied his voice seemed a note deeper. "If you're lousy in bed, I didn't notice any sign of it on this couch just now. You certainly had me in a state of high expectation."

"That was . . ." She darted him a look. "You're awfully good at . . . at foreplay, aren't you?"

"Foreplay?" Stephen shook his head, a brief, rueful smile twisting his features. "Janie, that wasn't foreplay. Or at least I wasn't thinking of it in any such technical terms. I was just loving you. I wanted to go on loving you, only you made me stop."

"You should thank me. If we'd gone on, it would just have been another failure."

She heard him inhale. "Is that really what you think?"

"That's what I know."

"How? How do you know?" Suddenly Stephen's dark eyes were shrewd. "After your divorce, did you try to have sex with other men?"

Vehemently, Jane shook her head. "Not the way you make it sound. I didn't go around looking to have an affair. But I did accept dates from time to time."

"And?"

Now when she looked at him sideways her blue eyes were resentful. "You know what men want? It might start out with a few kisses, but before long it's . . ."

"What was happening between us?" he said, finishing the sentence for her.

"Yes." The admission hissed between her teeth.

"And it didn't work?"

"No. It never worked. I would just freeze up. It wasn't long before I realized that Ward was right, there really is something wrong with me."

As Stephen contemplated the woman before him he was torn by a bewildering mix of emotions. She'd obviously been through hell and he felt sorry as well as concerned for her. But blended with that concern was a perverse but undeniable pleasure. Part of him was glad that she'd never climbed the heights of passion with Ward Cowle or any other man. It was almost as if the fates had in some strange way saved her for him.

Forcing what he knew was a selfish and irrational reaction into the background, he leaned forward and began to gently massage her tense shoulders.

"Jane, relax. I'm not going to try and make love to you again. I just want to talk to you."

When she gazed back the expression on her face was tinged with suspicion. But what she saw in his eyes seemed to reassure her. "There's nothing more to say on the subject."

"Oh, yes. There's a great deal. We're friends, remember?"

They hadn't really been friends in a long time. But suddenly she wanted it to be true very badly. Now that she'd told him about herself, she was oddly relieved. Gradually her rigid shoulders sagged and she let her head droop forward slightly so that Stephen could rub away the tight kinks in her neck.

"Janie, is this why you haven't accepted any dates around here? Because you're afraid?"

"Yes," she admitted. "It doesn't matter so much in a city where if things go wrong between you and a man you never need to see him again. In a small town like this . . ." She paused. "I just don't want to make any mistakes. Starting fresh here is too important to me."

"I see." Stephen's brows drew together and he gazed at the back of her bent head. "What was wrong between you and your husband?"

"I don't know. He said I wasn't responsive. And it's true, I wasn't. I tried to be, but I didn't really feel it."

Stephen was thoughtful for a moment. "Were you a virgin when you married?"

"Yes." She gave a dry little laugh. "I know it's hard to believe in this day and age. But I was."

"I believe it." Stephen's hands moved down to her shoulders again, and she sighed as their magic strength seemed to drain away some of her tension. "How about Ward? How experienced was he?"

She was startled by the question. "I don't know. He never discussed that with me."

"My guess is not very."

"What difference does it make?" She'd never talked so frankly to anyone before in her life. She could hardly believe that she was doing it now.

"A great deal," Stephen answered her question. "Jane, you must know that sexually men and women respond differently."

"I . . . I've read a few books." She felt her cheeks heat up again.

Stephen chuckled. "Reading is fine, but it doesn't compare with 'hands-on' experience, so to speak."

Unamused by the little joke, Jane turned her head. "I bet you've had plenty of that."

"Enough. But we're not talking about me. We're

talking about you, remember?" He squeezed her shoulder reassuringly and then went back to massaging it. "When you got married you were very young. You were shy and innocent and needed special treatment. It sounds to me as if you and Ward weren't suited and misunderstood each other on many different levels. What you take to be your sexual failure was just one of those misunderstandings. He needed to woo you more gently, and you needed to know how to help him do it."

Jane sighed deeply. Maybe Stephen was right, but all at once she was too tired to even attempt to make sense of what he was saying. Did it matter what the reason for the ruin of her marriage was? She had failed—miserably. "It's getting awfully late. I should go home," she managed to say.

Stephen's hand paused. "Why?"

"Why what?"

"Why go home?" As easily as if he were manipulating a child, he turned her toward him. "There's no reason for you to go home. Stay here with me."

Dumbfounded, Jane stared at him. He looked so solid and real sitting back against the couch with the warm light from the fire flickering over his lean features. His dark eyes studied her with open concern. Suddenly she felt a crazy impulse to lay her head against his shoulder. "I . . . I can't just not go home," she murmured.

"Why not?" He leaned forward and cradled her cheek between his warm palms. "Jane, there are three days before classes resume. If you go back to your apartment, how are you going to spend that time?"

Mostly alone, she thought. Aloud, she said, "I promised Carlie I'd baby-sit Davy tomorrow."

"You can call in the morning and tell her you can't make it. She'll find someone else."

That was true. Yet, Jane found herself unable to respond to Stephen's unexpected invitation.

As if he could read her mind and understood her dilemma, he smiled and gently tucked a strand of hair that had fallen over her forehead behind her ear. "Jane, we're both alone. We're both lonely in our different ways. You need help and I can offer it. Stay here with me."

"What . . . what do you mean?"

"Nothing that you need to be frightened about. Do you trust me?"

Jane couldn't tear her gaze away from his. She did trust him. It made no sense, but all her instincts told her to believe whatever he said. And since her brain didn't seem to want to work anymore, all she had to rely on was instinct. "Yes," she said, sounding even to her own ears as docile as a sleepy child.

Tenderly, his hand once more smoothed back her hair. "Good. You've made the right decision. And if you feel differently in the morning, I'll understand and take you back, no questions asked. But, right now, let me show you where you can sleep."

Gently, he lifted her to her feet and then led her up the stairs to a small bedroom. When he switched on the overhead light she could see immediately that it was the guest room and that it was unused. The wallpaper was an old-fashioned pattern of cabbage roses, and the bed under the slanted eaves was covered with a spotless white chenille spread.

"I'll put clean towels and a new toothbrush in the bathroom," Stephen told her after she'd looked around.

Shyly, her gaze flittered to his. "Where will you sleep?"

"Across the hall."

Her expression became quizzical. "Stephen, I shouldn't be doing this. I should make you take me home."

"Why?"

"Because I . . . I don't know exactly what you have in mind, but I don't want to start an affair or anything like that."

"Shhh." He leaned forward and gently pressed his lips against her forehead. The affectionate gesture soothed rather than frightened her. "Janie," he whispered. "Don't worry about it. Nothing's going to happen that you don't want or aren't ready for. Just relax for now and stay with me. I promise that everything will be okay."

Jane knew that acquiescence was irrational. But to another part of her his words made eminent good sense. What was the point of going back to her empty apartment? "All right," she agreed on a sigh.

He squeezed her hand. "I'll see you in the morning." Then, halfway turned toward the door, he paused and glanced back. "It's just occurred to me. I don't have any pajamas to offer you. The best I can do is a T-shirt."

"That'll be fine."

He looked vaguely uncomfortable. Then, shrugging, he disappeared through the door. A moment later he came back with a neatly folded square of red cotton knit material.

"It's the only one I have that's long enough," he explained apologetically as he laid it on the bed.

When he was gone and had closed the bedroom door behind him, Jane picked the fabric up and shook it out. Then her eyes widened. The shirt was long enough to reach her knees, but that wasn't what was making her stare. This garment, like so many other of Stephen's T-shirts, bore a legend. It read, "I will never be a party to lustful acts—unless you ask."

For several seconds her expression was frozen. Then, abruptly, she sat down on the bed and started to laugh. Clutching the scarlet material to her breast, she laughed until tears rolled out of her eyes and down her cheeks.

Ten minutes later Stephen stood in his darkened room staring out the window at the wave-tossed lake and listening to the howl of the wind. Reflectively, he lit a cigarette, an indulgence he allowed himself only infrequently these days. Where was this going to lead? he wondered. He couldn't even be sure himself what he really wanted. He only knew that there was a kind of inevitability about the situation developing between himself and Janie. It was a script that had to be acted out. And whatever his role demanded, he would give it his all.

CHAPTER SIX

Jane opened her eyes. It was morning, but the thin, gray light filtering through the window opposite the bed suggested that either it was very early or it was going to be another overcast day. When she glanced at her watch she was amazed to find that it read almost nine o'clock. Normally she woke up at seven, so despite the strange bed, she'd certainly managed to sleep well.

Of course it had been a while before she'd finally dropped off. For a long time she'd lain awake thinking about what had happened on Stephen's couch and about the strangeness of spending the night alone with him in his rented house.

She'd be sensible and go home this morning, she told herself. With that in mind, she pushed back the covers and swung her legs over the edge of the bed. Glancing down at the outrageous red T-shirt clinging to her breasts and bunched around her thighs, she grinned. Was Stephen still asleep? she wondered.

That question was answered when she pushed her bedroom door open a crack and wrinkled her nose. The delicious aroma of freshly brewing coffee wafted up the staircase. And she could hear the sound of someone moving around below in the kitchen. So he was up and fixing breakfast. Grabbing her clothing from the chair next to the bed, she scooted across the hall to the bathroom.

Ten minutes later, dressed, her face innocent of makeup, her hair neatly pulled back in a long braid that hung down her back, Jane made her way downstairs. As she approached the source of the noise, more appealing fragrances assaulted her nostrils. Bacon? Pancakes? After the scene in front of the fire last night, she was a little shy about seeing Stephen again. But the fact that he was going to so much trouble for her benefit eased some of her uncertainty.

"Whatever it is, it smells wonderful," she announced cheerily as she came through the entry.

Stephen was flipping pancakes on a griddle. When he saw her he put on a disappointed look. "You're up too soon. Go back upstairs and take your clothes off."

"What?"

"I was going to bring you breakfast in bed."

"Breakfast in bed?" Jane raised an eyebrow. "Well, in that case, I'm glad I woke up. I wouldn't have cared to receive company in that T-shirt of yours."

"So you did wear it. I wondered if you would." Grinning, he turned back to the stove.

"It was either that or sleep naked."

In the act of flipping another pancake, he missed and the doughy, half-cooked circle landed on the floor. "You just used the magic word," he remarked as he bent to scrape up the ruined food.

Jane laughed, but privately she wondered what on earth had possessed her to say something so provocative. To cover her discomfiture, she offered to take over at the stove. Stephen accepted, and while he poured the juice and coffee she finished the rest of the pancakes. When the food was ready they carried it out to the dining room and had a leisurely breakfast in the same setting where they'd enjoyed Thanksgiving dinner the day before.

"I really have to go home. I can't stay," she insisted as she leaned back to enjoy her second cup of coffee.

"Why not?"

"You said if I wanted to go back today, you wouldn't ask any questions."

"You should know better than to believe anything I say. Of course I'm going to try and talk you out of it. Listen, Jane, students have gone home for the holiday and classes don't start again until Monday. Give me one good reason why you can't keep me company for a while longer."

"I promised Carlie I'd baby-sit."

The expression on Stephen's face was choirboy angelic. "Just before you came down I called her and told her you couldn't make it."

"What?" Jane put down her cup. "Stephen, for God's sake!"

"I explained to her I needed you for rehearsals."

"Oh sure! You know what she's going to think, don't you?"

"That I'm an ogre, what else?" He smiled innocently, but with his sparkling dark eyes, there was more than a little of the devil about him.

Jane shook her head in exasperation, not sure what to do next. Part of her was angry at his high-handedness, but another part was secretly pleased. Even though she knew she really ought to leave, she didn't want to. What could it hurt to enjoy Stephen's company awhile longer?

He leaned forward and refilled her cup. "Janie, don't go scuttling back to your little cave. Stick around and see what happens next. What harm will it do?"

Maybe none, maybe a lot. She didn't know the answer. "All right," she finally said. "I'll stay for a little while. But I really have to get back before nightfall, Stephen. I really do."

Breakfast seemed to go on forever. Lingering over a third cup of coffee, they talked about a million different things—personalities around campus, the latest national news, current Broadway shows. It didn't seem to matter that outside the weather looked foreboding. In the comfortable little dining room, the atmosphere was cozily intimate.

"What are we going to do all day?" Jane demanded, holding out her cup for yet another refill.

"I don't know," Stephen admitted cheerfully. "Cleaning up after breakfast will probably take the rest of the morning. After that, if there's any time before lunch, we can run through some more numbers."

"Lunch?" Jane made a face. "After all this food, I doubt I'll want any."

Stephen suddenly looked smug. "Oh, when I get through with you, you'll want some."

At Jane's inquiring look he explained, "I know a very good way of working up an appetite. Why don't we venture out into the fresh air and take a nice, long healthy walk?"

His guest's bright blue eyes began to sparkle. "As a matter of fact, I've been around here before. I know of a mountain trail that leads up to a wonderful secluded lake."

Stephen nodded. "Crystal Lake. Your mission, should you choose to accept, Ms. Cowle, is to hike up there with me this afternoon."

While they cleared the table Jane laughingly

agreed to the challenge. But before they could start out, there was yet another challenging mission waiting for them in the kitchen. Stephen was a more than adequate cook, but he'd left an overwhelming trail of dirty dishes behind him.

"Are you always this messy?" she wanted to know.

"Only when I'm trying to impress a beautiful lady with my culinary skill. But not to worry," he added cheerfully. "I know we're going to make a great cleanup team."

It was more than an hour before the kitchen was tidy again. But that was partly because Stephen spent so much time distracting Jane and making her laugh. While she grimaced and rolled her eyes he produced a seemingly endless series of puns and one-liners. Then he showed off his juggling skill, keeping three cups flying from hand to hand until he finally dropped one. After she swept up the broken pieces he got out two different brands of paper towels and insisted that Jane watch while he demonstrated their virtues.

"See, Fluffo towels absorb a whole quarter cup of dish soap mixed with coffee grounds before they dissolve into a gooey green acid that will eat through ceramic tile."

"Gee, Mr. Science!" Jane shook her head. "I can't believe you actually went out and bought them just to test that out."

"I have an inquiring mind. Besides, it's things like this that keep you crazy. And that's the only way to be. Don't you agree?"

Jane nodded her assent. "A person certainly has to be a bit demented to hang around with the likes of you."

Despite his joking around, they really were a

good team. While he washed, she dried. "I wouldn't want you to get dishpan hands," he explained with mock sobriety.

"How about your hands?"

"If you're really worried about them, you can hold them in front of the fire tonight."

Sobering, Jane remembered the scene that had led up to her spending the night. Her expression clouded. "Stephen . . ."

"Don't say another word." He thrust the dishcloth at her. "Just hum Caitlin's fulfillment aria. I'll try and whistle the accompaniment."

Starting to laugh again, she put her hands on her hips. "You always were a terrible whistler."

"Not anymore. It's taken years of dedicated practice, but now I can pucker up like a bird. You'll see."

He was telling the truth about his improved ability to whistle, and by noon, as he filled a thermos and she assembled sandwiches to take along on their hike, Jane was properly awed. "Whatever made you want to learn to whistle 'The Minute Waltz'?"

"I was challenged at a party."

She eyed him thoughtfully. "Must have been some party."

Grinning easily, he screwed on the top of the stainless-steel container and placed it in his knapsack. "Hollywood parties can go on for days and crazy things sometimes happen at them in the wee, bleary hours of the morning. Believe me, a whistling contest is nothing."

She could believe that. And she could also believe that Stephen, without in any way compromising his own integrity, fit right into the Hollywood social scene. He'd never had any trouble charming everyone he met. Just as right now he was effortlessly charming her. The thought made her shoot him a guarded glance. But in only minutes he had her chuckling again, caution forgotten.

When the dishes were finally rinsed and put away and they'd slipped into their jackets, Stephen unearthed a drawer full of winter woolens. "Red for you and blue for me," he said, perching a scarlet cap at a jaunty angle on Jane's blond head. A few minutes later, bundled in scarves and mittens, they set off on their hike.

Though the wind had died, the sun had yet to appear. The sky, blanketed by pearly layers of clouds, hung low over the barren architecture of the leafless trees.

"I think it might snow," Stephen remarked, adjusting his stride to accommodate her shorter steps as they strolled along the road that circled the perimeter of Lake Dunmore.

Not long after they'd left the asphalt for the leaf-carpeted mountain path that led upward to Crystal Lake, the first sparse snowflakes began to drift down. A half an hour later the two hikers made it to the top of the steep path and began to walk down toward the small lake, which was set into the mountain's crest like a round, perfect jewel.

"Even though it's more gray than blue right now, it's still beautiful," Jane commented when they stood at the water's edge.

Stephen smiled down at her. "When it's reflecting a clear sky it's the same shade of sapphire as your eyes."

The compliment made Jane's cheeks go pink, and she looked away, hoping that he would ascribe their heightened color to the chilly air.

"Can I tempt you now?"

"Tempt me?"

"With coffee and sandwiches?" His teeth flashed and she knew he was teasing her.

"A hot drink, yes. Food, no."

They walked along the water's edge until they found a flat rock sheltered by a thick stand of tree trunks. After they settled themselves on it Stephen filled a cup for her. As she sipped gratefully at the steamy beverage she looked about, taking in all the details of the outdoor scene. Being with Stephen seemed to heighten all her senses. That had been particularly true the night before when he'd started to make love to her. But it was almost as true now. Here, sitting next to him in this beautiful, secluded spot, she felt as if her vision were sharper, her hearing keener, her sense of smell more refined. The gaunt shapes of the leafless trees reaching toward the muffled gray of the sky seemed to jam her vision. The damp air from the lake filled her lungs and made her skin tingle as if it were being stroked by frosty fingers.

The snowflakes were coming thicker now, and on impulse she lifted her face and let them dust her cheeks and forehead. "Mmmm, good," she murmured, licking one off her lips.

When she raised a mittened hand to brush away the flakes that had become tangled in her eyelashes, Stephen captured her hand in his. "No, let me," he said deeply. Then, to her confusion, she felt his warm mouth against her lowered lids.

"Oh, Stephen!" she murmured when at last she was able to open her eyes.

His face was only inches away and there was a tender smile quirking the corners of his mouth. "You can't have any idea how pretty you are right now. You don't look any older than you did when I first met you."

"Sometimes I wish I could go back to those days. I'd do a lot of things differently."

His expression was suddenly serious. "Like what?"

Her gaze captured by his, Jane considered the question. Suddenly she knew what he was asking. Her mind cast back to the night ten years ago when they'd parted. What would have happened if she'd gone with him? It was the first time she'd ever asked herself that. Would she have been any happier with Stephen in California than she had been with Ward in Boston? Jane shook her head. No, Stephen had been too young to make such a commitment then. And from what she knew of his life, she doubted that she would have fit in any better with his Hollywood friends than she had with the people her ex-husband had wanted to impress.

Instead of answering directly, Jane said, "What happened in my past will always be part of me. But it's the future I want to think about. It's the decisions I make from here on out that are really important."

"Smart lady." Turning away, Stephen opened his pack and then casually proffered a foil-wrapped package. "And speaking of important decisions, are you sure you won't have one of these sandwiches? After we've walked all the way around the lake, you'll need strength to get back down the mountain."

"Well . . ." Jane smiled. "Maybe I'll take half."

By the time they did return to the house, shadows were lengthening around its windows and a layer of snow iced the roof. Flakes were falling much more heavily and the wind had picked up enough to create swirling little eddies of white powder. Stephen speculated that sometime later that night there might be a real snowstorm, and Jane agreed.

"Maybe you'd better take me back home now," she said after they'd stripped off their coats and he'd set about laying another fire in the fireplace. "I wouldn't want to get snowed in."

"You don't have to worry about that. My station wagon has four-wheel drive." He glanced back at her over his shoulder. She was standing directly behind him rubbing her hands to get the circulation going again. The walk down the mountain had been considerably chillier than when they'd gone up. He eyed her assessingly, his dark scrutiny intent and filled with questions. "You don't really want to go back to your apartment, do you?"

Jane went very still, her eyes fixed on Stephen while she struggled to find an answer to his question. His kneeling position in front of the hearth made the breadth of his shoulders in the red plaid flannel shirt he wore even more of a sharp contrast to the lean jean-clad hips below his narrow waist. Her eyes skipped back up to his half-turned face. With his skin still ruddy from the cold outside, he looked the picture of hard, healthy masculinity. Something stirred deep within her. Her fingers itched to reach out and touch him and she felt even more confused. "No," she heard herself say in a low voice.

"I didn't think so. Then stay. You know you'll be all right with me, don't you?"

"Yes," she said, although she wasn't entirely sure that was true.

"Then stay."

Despite the uncertainty still gnawing in her mind, she knew the decision had been made and said no more. While he turned back to work on the fire, she went into the kitchen, where she made cocoa. A few minutes later Stephen joined her. Companionably, they sat by the window sipping the hot, sweet beverage and looking out at the gathering darkness.

"Do you want to do a little work at the piano?" he asked.

"Yes, why not?"

The only illumination in the living room now was the flickering light from the fireplace and the soft glow cast by the lamp which Stephen had switched on next to the piano. For more than an hour they rehearsed a number, Jane's high, clear voice piercing the shadows around them with arrows of what seemed to Stephen like unbearable sweetness. When she grew tired he led her to the couch and brought her a glass of wine.

As they each sipped from their glasses they didn't say much to each other. But there was a feeling of communion between them that was as tangible as any words.

"You're going to spend the night, aren't you?"

"Yes." Jane's thick lashes shielded her lowered eyes.

"Do you mind wearing that T-shirt to bed again?" her host teased gently.

"The one about lustful acts?" She shot him a shy look. "No, I don't mind."

"Good." He reached over and caught her hand. "It's true, you know. Even though it goes against the grain, I'll be a perfect gentleman until you say the word. But that's all it will take, Jane—just one word. I'd like to make love to you tonight."

She lifted her blue gaze to his. Why not? she asked herself. She was thirty years old and she wanted him. Why not? She'd already warned him it might be disappointing. It wasn't as if she'd tried to deceive him into thinking she was some sort of sexpot. "Do you wear a T-shirt when you go to bed?" she inquired inconsequentially.

"No, but I'm wearing one now under the plaid flannel."

"What does it say?"

Stephen's baritone was husky. "Unbutton it and find out."

Jane hesitated. Then, with the dreamy movements of a somnambulist, she set her glass down and reached forward. She could see a bit of white just above the place where his shirt closed at his throat, so she knew he really was wearing a T-shirt. Above its neckline a few strands of crisp black hair showed, and Jane remembered how his chest was matted with them. Very conscious of the heat from his body, and with fingers that were only slightly unsteady, she slid open the two top buttons. Still nothing showed but white cotton knit.

"Where's the message?"

"It's a little lower. Keep going."

The look she cast him was doubtful. "How much lower?"

Though his body remained perfectly still, his strong hands idle at his sides, Stephen's eyes sparkled with masculine mischief. "Only a little lower, Miss Muffet. You're still perfectly safe."

Quickly, Jane undid the next button. She could now see the tops of a few black letters, but it was still impossible to make out their message. Her gaze fell to the next button. It was only inches above the place where his jeans rode low on his hips and snapped over his flat, hard belly.

Clearly entertained by her predicament, Stephen said, "Go ahead, undo it. I won't bite you." He grinned. "Unless you ask."

Shooting him a look that was faintly resentful and amused at the same time, Jane did as he bade and pushed open the shirt. Now she could read its legend clearly. In wide black letters it said, "Hug me!"

The corners of her mouth started to lift. She looked up into Stephen's face. He was smiling, too, his dark eyes alight with tender laughter. "Well," he said, opening his arms wide, "can't you follow instructions?"

It seemed the most natural thing in the world. Moving across the few inches that separated them on the couch, Jane wrapped her arms around his wide chest and laid her cheek against his shoulder. He felt so good, so strong and solid. But it wasn't just that. She loved the feel of him for a myriad of reasons. The curls that spilled over his forehead, his crooked, dancing smile, the texture of his brown skin, the way the sound of his voice seemed to make each of her nerve ends stand at attention—it was all part of a whole man that to Jane was infinitely appealing, infinitely seductive.

He wrapped his arms around her and held her close. Then he tipped her chin up and kissed her lips. "Jane, I want to make love to you tonight. Will you let me?"

She gazed searchingly up at him. "Stephen, I'd like to, but I'm not very good at this."

"You weren't listening." He nipped at the lobe of her ear and then whispered, "I didn't ask you to be good. I asked you to let *me* make love to *you.*"

"I don't want you to be disappointed."

"I don't intend to be. Janie, I can feel you tensing up." His mouth moved along the line of her jaw and then once more settled lightly on her lips. "Just relax," he murmured against them. "Just relax and enjoy." As he kissed her his hand massaged her shoulders and then the curve of her back, seeming to find and gratify every sensitive spot along her spine. The kiss went on and on, and gradually, under the gentle but persistent persuasion of Stephen's lips and hands, she did relax. When at last his mouth left hers she felt limp and compliant.

Stephen drew back and gazed at her thoughtfully. "Let's do this right."

She imagined by that he meant to lead her up to his bedroom. Instead, he got up, took a soft wool blanket out of the chest behind the couch, and unfolded it on the floor between the fireplace and the coffee table. When it was neatly spread he beckoned for her to join him.

Jane hesitated. "You don't overpower your women with hot kisses before seducing them?"

"Seduction is not what I have in mind. I want to make love to you, and I want you to be willing. No games."

Levelly, he met and held her gaze, waiting for her to decide. She swallowed and then got down on the blanket next to him.

"Good girl." He gave her a smile that was an odd mixture of sweetness and triumph. "Now, let me explain something to you about lovemaking." He began to undo the braid at the back of her head, carefully combing his fingers through it to loosen the strands. "In many ways it's the ultimate act of trust. You can trust me, Jane. And the first thing you can trust me with is your protection. I'll take care of everything."

She stared at him, absorbing that. "You have something here?"

"Yes, I do. Life is unpredictable for a bachelor, so I generally keep something around. But I won't lie to you, when you came out here I hoped for this.

Don't get me wrong. You can decide at any time that you want to change your mind. But mine is made up. I've wanted you for a long time."

How long? she wondered. But there was no opportunity to ask, for even as he spoke Stephen was once more gathering her to him. Though she'd stiffened up again slightly, it wasn't long before his drugging kisses and stroking hands once more eased her tension. He didn't pressure her, merely made her know that she was desired.

The only light in the room now was the warm glow from the fireplace. To Jane, the mesmerizing flicker of its red and gold flames seemed a part of everything else—the rhythmic glide of Stephen's hands, his unhurried, persuasive kisses, the heat rising between them.

"Getting warm in here," he said, echoing her thoughts. "I don't think we need all these clothes. What do you think?"

He drew back a few inches so that he could read her expression more easily. Slowly she shook her head.

Stephen grinned. "Unless you start to kick and scream, I'll interpret that as a sign of agreement." Matter-of-factly, his hands found the hem of her sweater and rolled it upward. "This has got to go."

As he carefully pulled the garment over her head and off her arms, Jane felt almost like a child being undressed for bed by a solicitous father. It occurred to her that if she was going to change her mind about this, now would be a good time to do it.

But Stephen's sweet, undemanding kisses had made her feel languorous and receptive. There was nothing frightening about this gentle, friendly seduction. She didn't want to draw back, she wanted to see what would happen next.

It was exactly the reaction Stephen had hoped for. He considered that she'd been alarmed last night because he'd gone too fast. This time would be different. If it killed him, he'd keep the primitive urgency of his physical reaction to her in check and take this very slowly and very carefully.

Beneath her sweater Jane wore only a cotton bra. She expected Stephen to take that off next. But instead he sat up, slipped his arms out of his plaid shirt, and then removed the T-shirt that had gotten all this started. It came as a shock to her to see his upper body nude. She'd seen it before, but now, with the firelight playing over his torso, glistening on the black hair on his chest, he stirred feelings that disturbed and excited her. His shoulders were broad and well-muscled, and she could see the sinewy strength of his arms.

"You used to be so skinny," she commented.

"I was a scrawny kid," he agreed. "But for years now I've been eating my Wheaties and working out in a gym. I may not be Charles Atlas, but no one's kicked sand in my face recently."

As he spoke he slid back down next to her and traced the line of her shoulder with a single, exploring finger. "You're thinner than you were in the old days."

"I used to be fat."

"Not true. You were pleasingly plump and oh so delicious-looking." His mouth came down on the point of her breast still covered by the thin cotton of her bra. When his tongue traced a damp circle through the material, she shivered and arched toward him. "You're still delicious," he said huskily. His hands went around to her back and unsnapped the bra. "I'm bare above the waist and you should be too. Fair is fair."

She giggled. "It's not the same thing, as you very well know." Her laughter died in her throat when his mouth returned to her naked breast. The little tugging movements of his lips felt so good. It was as if they awakened tingling threads that reached down deep within her body. Though Ward had kissed her breasts, his mouth had been harsh, sometimes even hurtful. Stephen's was tender and knowing, as though he understood exactly what felt good. How could he know? she wondered vaguely.

But it was impossible to reflect on the question. There were too many other sensations crowding in on her mind. Though Stephen's mouth continued to adore her upper body, his hands wandered lower. She was only dimly aware when he undid the closure on her slacks, but when she felt his fingers on the smooth skin of her stomach, she shivered with anticipation. In the next moment that anticipation was gratified as his hand slipped beneath the elastic of her panties and began to touch and caress her in ways that made her hips involuntarily undulate beneath his.

Her own hands fluttered over his back, coming to rest at last on his lean waist. She wanted to return some of the pleasure and excitement that he was showing her. Ward had always dragged her hand to his impatient center of desire and clamped it there. Unbidden, she was too shy to touch Stephen in that way. Yet she felt the need to reciprocate some of his attentions. Hesitantly, her fingers began to dig beneath the waistband of his jeans.

She felt him shudder. Then suddenly he rolled over on his back and took her with him so that she found herself sprawled on top of his hard body, staring down into the simmering depths of his dark eyes. "If you'll unsnap my jeans, I'll be forever in your debt, young lady," he whispered thickly, one hand cupping her breast while his thumb lightly grazed the stiffened nipple.

He made her want to laugh and excited her all at the same time. Suddenly emboldened, she whispered back, "If I do, what will you give me?"

"Wait and see. Something you'll like, I guarantee that."

She was beginning to believe he might be right. Pulling away slightly, her fingers went down to his jeans, unsnapped them, and began to pull down the zipper.

"Careful," Stephen groaned. "Easy does it."

She could see why he'd cautioned her, and the realization was rather daunting. He'd said she could draw back from this experiment any time. What if she asked him to stop now? Would he be angry, call her a tease, try to force her? Before she could consider the consequences of her words, she found herself asking the question:

"What would happen if I wanted to stop now?"

He put his hands around her waist and rolled again so that he was once more looking down at her, taking in the pouting fullness of her naked breasts, the silken sheen of her skin in the ruddy light. "It would certainly put a damper on my evening. I'd probably have to spend the rest of the night reciting baseball scores in a cold shower. Would you do that to a sweet guy like me?"

Jane brought her hand up to the crisp hair surrounding one of his flat nipples and gently massaged the tiny nub of flesh. "No."

Stephen's white teeth flashed. "Then let's proceed along the same lines we've been pursuing so far. I think it's time we got naked. What do you say?"

"Okay."

"Just the reply I was hoping for. However did you guess?"

Without waiting for an answer to the obvious, he got up on his knees and began to tug her slacks off. With his jeans unzipped below his bare chest and his desire very evident beneath the white Jockey shorts, he looked so sexy he took Jane's breath away.

In the process of divesting her of her slacks, he managed to pull her panties most of the way down her hips so that they were only a wisp across her thighs. Realizing that she was now totally vulnerable, she sucked in her breath. Stephen paused to study her, his gaze taking in every detail.

"I won't say 'Gawd, you're beautiful!' because you'd probably laugh at me. But it's true, Janie. You're a lovely woman. You deserve better than you've had so far. You probably deserve better than me. But you'll have no regrets about tonight. That I promise." Leaning forward, he kissed her along the line of the creased panties and then slid them down over her thighs. When they were off completely he removed his own clothing so that for the first time she saw him entirely naked.

She hadn't realized he'd be so beautiful—or so threatening. His body was as long and lean as a distance runner's, every muscle clearly defined. The black hair that matted his chest also dusted his sinewy calves and grew in an arrow to his groin. It was what Jane saw there that she found daunting. Ward had been frightening to look at, but Stephen was even more alarming. How would she accommodate him? And how was he managing to be so patient with her when he was so aroused? she wondered. Ward had never lingered like this over sexual encounters or been playful. Everything had always happened very fast—too fast, Jane realized.

"Don't be afraid." Stephen soothed as he sank down beside her once again. "It's going to be all right. I promise."

"How can you promise a thing like that?" Her voice was a husky breath that sounded unfamiliar even to her own ears.

"Because I know just what to do. Now, close your eyes and let me make you want me."

"I do already." It was true. There was a receptive ache in her groin that she recognized held more desire than Ward had ever aroused in all the years of their marriage.

"You're beginning to," Stephen contradicted in a thickened voice. "But not anywhere near enough. I'll know when the time is right, and so will you." He kissed her eyelids shut and then his mouth began to wander delicately over her face and throat. But it was his hands rather than his lips that occupied most of her attention. With the flat of his palm, he stroked down the quivering length of her body, pausing only when he reached the juncture between her thighs. She trembled when his fingers began to weave an erotic pattern there and she whispered a faint protest.

"Shhh," he murmured huskily. "You like that, don't you? Your body is telling me you do. Admit it."

"Yes." Sensations of tingling heat were shooting up and down her legs and centering themselves low in her belly.

"Then be still and let me love you. Don't try and do anything. Just be still."

Resistance was impossible. Relaxing in his arms, she abandoned the last of her inhibitions and let him do what he would. While his mouth caressed her breasts his hand seemed to discover all her secrets. Jane moaned. A fiery knot was growing and spreading through the core of her body. It was produced, Jane knew, by the rhythmic motions of Stephen's alarming, exciting hand. Paradoxically, his delicious caresses made her feel as if she were aflame and at the same time as if she were dissolving. "What are you doing to me?" she gasped.

"Just loving you," he whispered back, claiming her soft mouth with his firm lips so that she could say no more. While his tongue invaded her so did his knowing fingers. But Jane was beyond protest at this new intimacy. Once again her body was that of a stranger's, awash in unfamiliar sensations that left her feeling both helpless and strangely triumphant.

Willingly, her thighs parted, letting him work his kindling magic. It was as if every cell of her being were alive in an entirely new dimension. And Stephen was all part of it, his lips on her, his probing tongue, the texture of his smooth, velvety hide, the feel of his hair-roughened legs tangling with hers. His caresses grew far less leisurely, and at last she sensed some of the urgency he was restraining. As his hands played on her body with imperative sensitivity, she could feel his masculinity pressed hard against her hip.

It was all part of a sensual tapestry so overwhelming that she had to close her eyes. But behind her shuttered lids, fires still glowed—fiercely dancing flames that were part of the incendiary attentions Stephen was giving her. The flames grew and leapt until she was engulfed by them, her whole body a shimmering explosion of pleasure.

"Oh, oh Stephen!"

"That's it," he whispered in fierce triumph. "That's it. Just let go."

She clung to his waist, urging him toward her. He made her wait while he opened a silvery packet. But then he came to her and she enfolded him between her legs. Moments earlier she'd wondered how she could accommodate the size of his aroused masculinity. Now she wondered how she could go on enduring this emptiness. She ached for him, wanted him to fill her.

For Stephen there was no more hesitation. He'd said he'd know when she was ready, and he hadn't lied. Groaning his satisfaction with her eager response, he cupped her soft buttocks in his palms and lifted her toward him. Then she felt the satisfying, steely thrust as her body closed around his and they became one.

CHAPTER SEVEN

Jane didn't know what had awakened her. But suddenly her eyes were open and she was staring into the thick darkness. Stirring slightly, her leg encountered the warmth of another body, and she jerked back. But then she realized where she was—not in her bedroom or in the guest bed where she'd slept last night. She was in Stephen's room, sleeping next to him.

Her eyes strained, trying to make out his head resting on the pillow next to hers. She could hear the steady rise and fall of his breath. He was sleeping like a baby. But he was no baby, nor was he her old friend anymore. He was the man who'd become her lover, who in one galvanizing evening had freed her from a web of fears and inhibitions and who'd awakened a sensuality in her at which she'd never guessed.

As memories of what had happened a few hours earlier burst in her mind, Jane was suddenly wide awake and almost trembling with excitement. This was an important night in her life, perhaps the most important. On this night, in Stephen Hammond's arms, she'd truly become a woman. For the first time she'd experienced the ecstasy that was part of her birthright. And she hugged that exhilarating knowledge to herself.

All at once her senses were alert. Outside she could hear the whisper of the lake, and something else. Her ears strained and she turned her face toward the window. Through the edges of the drawn curtains there was a faint glow.

Fascinated, Jane pushed the covers away and slipped out of bed. She glanced back at her lover, but he seemed to be breathing as evenly as before, his sleep undisturbed. The air was chilly outside the bedclothes and Jane was naked. Luckily, when she touched the chair next to the bed, her hand fell on a velour bathrobe which Stephen had left draped there. Gratefully she slipped into it and then padded to the window.

When she moved the curtains to one side and peered out, she saw the source of the faint glow. The world outside was wrapped in a blanket of white. Fat flakes of snow thickened the air and silently drifted down to mantle the trees.

The sight seemed to catch at her throat. It was as if the snow were blessing her as well as the world outside, wiping away all the pain and failure of the past and promising that the future would be better. For a long time she stared out at it, tears gathering at the corners of her eyes.

Then she heard the springs creak under the mattress and sensed Stephen's presence. She could actually feel him walking toward her, even though his quiet feet made no sound on the polished floor.

"Jane?" His hand went to the back of her neck, massaging gently.

"It's snowing," she said inanely.

"Yes, I see."

"It's beautiful out there."

"As far as I'm concerned, it's beautiful in here

too." He turned her toward him and drew her close. "Is something wrong?"

"No, no, nothing's wrong." At this moment everything seemed absolutely right. "I just woke up and couldn't get back to sleep."

He was silent a moment, then undid the tie on the robe she wore, opened it, and closed the small distance between them so that their naked bodies touched at every point. "Come back to bed," he growled in her ear. "I know something that works for insomnia better than bedtime stories and warm milk."

"I wonder what that could be." Chuckling, she moved even closer so that her breasts were flattened against the hair on his hard chest.

"I don't intend to keep you guessing." He swept her up in his arms and carried her back toward the double bed at the other end of the room.

Jane clung to him. After just one brief night in Stephen's arms she felt transformed, like an altogether different woman. Before, she'd been hesitant about physical involvement, afraid of failure and disappointment. Now, she thrilled at the prospect of Stephen's body covering hers.

Already, she could feel her breasts tingling with excitement. Her skin, sensitized by the cool air, seemed to soak up his warmth. It eagerly took in other sensations as well, the masculine aroma that was uniquely his, his breath stirring stray tendrils on her forehead. As he pressed her close she was keenly aware of the texture of his crinkly chest hair against her swelling nipples. When he laid her on the mattress she reached up toward him, desiring the mastery of his lean, hard length more than she had ever desired anything in her life.

He came to her at once, his approach no longer

experimental but confident. Cupping her breasts in his hands, he kissed the straining nipples, hovering over each like a hummingbird attracted to nectar. The gentle suckling movements of his lips and tongue were electrifying.

"You need to tell me what feels good to you," he enjoined huskily.

Her brain wasn't working very well. She was hardly able to put together an answer. "What you're doing now is wonderful. It all feels good."

The laughter deep in his throat was part growl, part exclamation. "And this?"

His hand had found her most sensitive spot.

"Oh, yes!"

While his persistent fingers weaved patterns of enchantment she arched toward him. But she also felt the need to give back some of the magic he was bestowing. Shyly her hand went around his hip and stroked the tight roundness of his small, hard buttocks. Then, more shyly yet, her fingers slipped to the flat plain of his belly. She waited, but there was no objection from him, only an encouraging sound deep in his throat. She moved lower. What she found was imposing, but having already experienced his wonders, Jane was no longer intimidated.

At her delicate touch, Stephen shuddered and then groaned. "Oh, sweetheart, I love it! But if you do very much of that to me, I won't be able to wait."

"You don't need to wait." She knew that she was ready for his possession. Her need for him made her feel strong. For Jane it was a confirmation of her womanliness, a confirmation that had been a long time in coming.

With another groan, Stephen yielded to her enticements. Settling himself between her thighs, he captured her mouth and at the same time his supple hips thrust deeply. Invaded by his hot tongue and his even more imperative sex, she was his captive. Yet, he was hers. Eagerly her body welcomed his, glorying in the urgency she could feel exploding around her. She pushed herself against him so that he could capture her even more completely, and then she quivered at the fiery sensation.

A sigh of mutual satisfaction was lost between their hungry mouths. Stephen's hands gripped her hips and he began to move. His need was controlled at first, but she answered each driving invasion so ardently that they soon lost their measured rhythm and became feverish. She was no less passionate in her response. Clasping his waist and locking her thighs around him, she closed her eyes tight and became lost in a pattern of light and dark, of leaping flames and bursts of color.

When Stephen collapsed against her they were both breathing hard. For a long time they lay, thigh to thigh, silently stroking each other. Gradually their breathing became regular and their movements stilled. Just before they both drifted off to sleep, Stephen pulled up the blankets and kissed her mouth lingeringly.

"Good night, sweet Jane," he whispered.

But she was already lost to the world and in reply only snuggled closer to his warmth and smiled contentedly in her sleep.

When she awoke next it was Stephen who stood by the window looking out. He'd pulled on his jeans, but otherwise he was naked, his narrow waist and broad back modeled by the muted light. Jane lay very still under the covers studying the attractive picture he made and wondering what he would say to her. Mornings after were probably a routine matter for him. But for her this was something entirely new.

Sensing her gaze on him, he turned and smiled sweetly. "It's nothing but white out there. We're snowed in."

"I thought you said you had four-wheel drive."

"I do, but let's forget about that." He began to walk toward her. "I like the idea of having a beautiful woman trapped in my bed. Let's pretend we're stuck here for a few more hours. What do you say?"

Her blue eyes crinkled at the corners. "All right—as long as the food holds out."

He laughed and the mattress sagged under his weight as he sat down on its edge. "You look very pretty with your hair spilling all over the pillowcase. It's the color of sunshine."

"It needs a wash, and so do I."

"Well, since you're my guest, I'd better see to it that you get one. In fact"—he took her hand and tugged her out of bed—"I'll scrub you all over personally."

Laughing and blushing because she was naked, Jane allowed him to lead her down the hall to the bathroom. It was a large, old-fashioned room with linoleum on the floor and a claw-foot tub. But the tub had a shower head, and within minutes she and Stephen were standing breast to breast beneath its warm spray. On impulse, she locked her arms around his waist, lay her head on his hard, matted chest, and let the water fall over her.

For a while Stephen stood still and merely stroked her back, thinking how strange life was. When he'd first held Jane in his arms it had seemed like a dream. Now it was even more so, reality and fantasy blending and becoming indistinguishable. Opening his eyes, he looked down at Jane's slender curves. She was so lovely. Her hair, darkened by the water, lay against her back in a sleek queue that pointed down to her tiny waist. Below that her hips flared to a delicious feminine softness that Stephen's palms yearned to capture. Sliding his hands down, he splayed them around Jane's sleek buttocks and gently kneaded.

Soon his tender, reflective mood turned amorous and the temperature of his and Jane's water activities became steamy. As they twisted together beneath the heated downpour she once more forgot the world outside. There was only this moment, this man, and the thrilling sensations he was able to invoke in her.

But at last they ran out of hot water. The spray became chilly and Stephen was forced to turn it off. "You're developing goose bumps," he said solicitously as he helped Jane out of the tub. "We can't have that."

"What about you? Aren't you cold too?"

"Don't worry about me." He took a fluffy brown towel off the rack and began to rub her body with great care. "What we were doing in the shower just now probably raised my temperature to an all-time high."

Jane merely giggled, but privately she wondered if he meant any of the wonderful things he was saying. How many morning-after showers had he taken with other women? And had his temperature actually been any higher with her than it had with those other females?

Stephen didn't allow her much time to speculate about this. When she was dry he wrapped the towel around her torso, kissing the vee between her breasts before tucking the edge of the terry cloth in to hold it in place. "Enough of this hedonism," he said sternly. "Time to get dressed and plan our day."

"What did you have in mind?" Jane asked as they strolled back to his bedroom. Seemingly totally unself-conscious, Stephen wore his towel casually draped over his shoulder. There were fine drops of moisture glistening in his raven curls, and the faint sheen of moisture that still clung to his healthy hide made it hard for her to keep her eyes from drifting over him greedily.

Before answering her question, he frowned as though thinking deeply. "Well, we can have breakfast first, then a romp in the snow, then back to bed to warm up, then another romp in the snow, then back to bed to warm up, then . . ."

She poked him in the side with her elbow. "Be serious. We can't spend the whole day in bed."

"We can't? What are you trying to do? Ruin my Thanksgiving?"

Leaving her standing in the bedroom with her hands on her hips, he went downstairs to retrieve their scattered clothing. Then, like naughty children, they dressed each other, trading jokes that made less and less sense but seemed to grow funnier and funnier.

Breakfast was like that too. Everything they ate was delicious; everything they said was incredibly witty and utterly charming. When it was over they bundled up and left the house for the whiteness that still sheltered them from the outside world. It had finally stopped snowing and the sky had cleared. Now the sun shone down on what looked almost like a field of sparkling diamonds. Jane paused outside Stephen's front door to survey the fairy-tale beauty.

"It's gorgeous," she breathed. "Almost like stepping into another world." She smiled up into Stephen's face.

He smiled back at her. Jane's cheeks were pink, her eyes bright blue, her hair the color of buttercups beneath the red knit cap she wore. With one gloved finger he reached out and touched her cheek.

"Well, what's your pleasure? Shall we make a snowman or shall we be more ambitious and go for a fort?"

"Neither," Jane declared, skipping forward and plopping herself down on the ground with the joyful abandon of a ten-year-old. "Let's start with snow angels."

They played in the snow for more than an hour, producing a masterpiece of a snowman and stopping from time to time to pelt each other with snowballs. But finally, wet and shivering, they went back inside for hot cocoa.

Jane spread the coats, hats, and scarves out to dry and climbed the stairs to get a towel. Stephen went into the kitchen to put water on the stove. Up in his bedroom, she was just pulling off her wet socks when the phone rang.

"Get that, would you?" he called.

Obediently, Jane stretched to reach the phone on the bedside table and lifted the receiver to her ear. Then she heard his voice shouting up to her again.

"Never mind, I've got it."

She had to wait until she heard him say hello before she could hang up or the caller would be disconnected. She was just about to replace the receiver when she heard a breathy female voice say, "Stephen, I mean, Mr. Hammond?"

"Yes."

"This is Tina."

Jane's hand seemed to be glued to the phone. She knew she should put it down, but it was impossible to pull the thing away from her ear.

"Yes, Tina, what can I do for you?" Stephen replied.

"Well, I got back to town early, and I'm all alone here in the dorm with nothing to do and no one to talk to. While I was home I worked on that composition—you know, the one you said you'd look at again. And I was wondering, that is, would you mind if I dropped it off at your house this afternoon or later this evening so we could discuss it?"

There was a brief pause during which Jane held her breath. How is he going to get out of this one? she wondered. One sex-starved woman in his bedroom and another maneuvering to get her foot in his door!

"I'm afraid it will have to wait until Monday during office hours, Tina. I've got company."

"Oh."

There was a wealth of frustration and disappointment in that one syllable, and Jane couldn't keep the satisfied smile off her face. It slipped, however, when Tina hung up and Jane heard Stephen say, "Well, Janie, was I a good boy? Did I handle that okay?"

She could literally feel her ears turning red.

He chuckled. "Come on, sweetheart, don't play dead. I know you're there."

"All right," she said stiffly. "But you asked me to pick up the phone."

"Well, of course you could have put it down any time. But since you didn't, give me a candid opinion. Do I pass the dirty-old-man test?"

"I never accused you of being a dirty old man. You're not old."

He barked a laugh.

"I think you handled the situation beautifully," she added. "Just how many times a day does this sort of thing happen?"

"Often enough. I told you—the girls around here are damned aggressive. At least this one called first to make an appointment." He chuckled again and then the phone went dead. Jane was still staring down at it when she heard his feet on the stairs. A moment later he burst through the half-open door, his face lit by a wicked grin. "Why," he said, continuing the conversation as though it hadn't been interrupted, "should I want to lure Tina to my infamous bachelor pad when I've already trapped myself a gorgeous blonde?"

As he spoke he flung himself on the bed, and all at once Jane found herself crushed in a bear hug that nearly squeezed all the breath from her. Then she was neatly flipped on her back. While Stephen's hungry kiss silenced her laughing objections his hands busily unzipped her slacks, rolled up her sweater, and unhooked her bra.

"Stephen!" she managed to protest when at last his lips momentarily abandoned hers.

"Shhh! You're cold and need to be warmed up. I'm an excellent warmer-upper. Know all the right spots to heat." As he spoke he drew her sweater up over her head and then began tugging off her pants.

Jane giggled. But though she was amused, she was also excited, her body responding to Stephen's playful sexuality like a fireman to an alarm bell. In moments they were both naked and twined on the bed. Breathless, laughing, and instantly aroused, Jane ran her hands down the smooth, tight curve of her lover's buttocks and urged him toward her. But Stephen refused to be rushed. He insisted first on nibbling and kissing all the places that were most sensitive to his caresses. With unerring accuracy, he found and teased every vulnerable secret that her body possessed. And only when she was melting with desire and almost begging for his possession did he join his body to hers in a fiery communion that left them both utterly satisfied.

As they lay in each other's arms Jane's gaze wandered over Stephen's body, taking in the well-formed, hair-dusted legs, the lean hips that had driven her to such a frenzy of sensation minutes earlier, and the hands with their long, sensitive fingers. How knowing those hands were, how able with the lightest touch to bring her body to a pitch of desire of which she'd never before even thought herself capable.

From where her head rested against his chest she glanced up at the underside of his jaw and then drew back a bit so that she could see his face. His eyes were half closed.

"You're a very good lover, aren't you?"

"What?" Stephen's eyes opened.

"I've never had sex with anyone but Ward, but I have a suspicion that you're better at this sort of activity than most men."

"Well, thank you, ma'am. I aim to please."

For reasons she didn't stop to examine, the light remark irked her. "How do you know so much about women? Where did you learn?" He hadn't had all this expertise ten years ago, she knew. Though she remembered that she'd responded to the kiss he'd forced on her when they were undergraduates, it had been awkward compared to his smooth lovemaking now. An awful lot must have occurred in the interim.

He was gazing down at her with his brows drawn

together. "Are you asking me where I learned how to make love?"

"Yes, I guess I am."

He laughed at her, a questioning edge on his amusement. "I read a lot."

But now that Jane had started down this track, she found that she didn't want to turn back. "You don't learn how to please a woman the way you just did me by reading a how-to book. As you pointed out earlier, it takes some hands-on experience."

"Yes, I guess it does." His lips twitched.

"So I'm curious. How did it happen for you? Ward was almost twenty-five when I married him, yet compared to you he was a clod in bed."

Stephen couldn't help but be pleased by that observation. "This is an odd conversation we're having."

"This is an odd weekend."

He twirled a strand of her fair hair around his index finger. "Yes, I guess it is. Okay, when I was in my early twenties I met a woman several years older. Margie had just been through a messy divorce and was lonely. In my way, I was lonely too."

"Do you mean that you had an affair with her?"

" 'Affair' isn't the right word. We lived together for a couple of years. We were friends and lovers with the emphasis on friends."

"What happened?"

"Neither of us ever expected it to be a permanent thing. She met another guy, someone she wanted to marry." Stephen put a hand behind his head and thought about Margie. With gentle patience, she'd taught him how to please her. Every bumbling youngster should have a Margie, he considered, and he would always be grateful to her.

"Were you unhappy when she left you?" Jane asked.

"No. It was time for us to split, and we both knew it. She decided that she was ready to try marriage again, and I was just glad that she found the right guy."

"But marriage wasn't what you wanted."

"No. I wasn't ready to make that sort of commitment."

Jane continued to study the underside of Stephen's jaw. Once again she asked herself if he was a perennial bachelor—the type of man who enjoyed a string of affairs but was incapable of a lasting relationship. Surely, living in Hollywood, he'd bedded many beautiful and sexually sophisticated women. How did she compare with them? Badly, no doubt. Her next statement was blurted out before she had a chance to censor it. "I imagine that compared to your other bedmates, I'm not exactly a hot tamale."

His chest rumbled with laughter. "Do you want to be a hot tamale?"

Suddenly irrationally indignant, she propped herself up on her elbow. "Well, I don't want you to remember this as being the most boring weekend of your life."

"Believe me, I won't." She was leaning over him, her face only a few inches from his, her hair falling in a gilded swath that grazed his cheek and lay in silken strands on his neck and shoulders. As his dark gaze melted into her blue one, Stephen's expression became serious, almost somber. Slowly he reached up, cupped the back of her head in his palm, and pulled her face down to his. The long, sensuous kiss he bestowed was gentle, tender. When he released her he whispered against her lips, "Janie, this has been the most exciting, fulfilling weekend of my life."

Though the words thrilled and pleased her, she couldn't believe them. "I think you must tell that to all your lady friends."

"No. I've said it only to you."

He looked so serious. But how could he really be telling the truth? "Why?" she whispered.

Like a caress, his gaze drifted over her cheeks, her mouth, farther down to her breasts, the pink tips of which grazed his chest. Then his eyes went back to hers. "Let me show you something."

While she watched curiously he rolled off the bed and, after pulling on his jeans, walked to the tall bureau near the window. After he'd opened a drawer and removed a small object from a box, he strode back to the bed. Sitting down on its edge, he opened her palm and dropped something cool and metallic into it.

"Recognize that?"

Jane stared down at the piece of jewelry in her hand. It was a broken silver chain with a small pendant in the shape of a musical note. Her grandmother had given it to her for her sixteenth birthday. "This was mine. Where did you get it?"

"Don't you remember how it was lost?"

With a small shock, she did remember. She'd lost it on that summer night ten years ago when Stephen tried to kiss her. Somehow it had been torn from her, and when she'd gone to look for it in the street the next morning, it hadn't been there.

"You kept the chain all these years? But why?"

"Can't you guess?" He shook his head. "Oh, Janie, during that summer I developed a crush on you that would have made a mountain avalanche seem puny. You didn't know it, did you?"

Her expression said it all. Her mouth was slightly open, her eyes stretched wide. "No."

"You didn't even guess?" He was amused, but unaccountably some of the old hurt surfaced as well. How could she have been so blind to the love and longing that had tormented him? he wondered.

"I knew there was something special between us —that we were really good friends, but . . ."

"But you refused to acknowledge it was anything more than that. I was a year younger than you so you thought of me as a kid, and you were too hung up on your precious Ward to see beyond your nose."

That was true, Jane acknowledged. At twenty she'd been too caught up in her own little fantasy of getting married and living happily ever after to acknowledge anything that seemed to threaten it.

Stephen sighed. "I knew that, of course. I knew it would only embarrass you if I told you how I felt. But it didn't stop me from wanting you. And it all came out that last night before I left. I attacked you, and you fled in terror."

"You didn't attack me. You kissed me."

"I kissed you, and you ran away." Stephen took the silver chain from her hand and dangled it between his fingers. "Until last night this was all I had left of you, so I kept it."

"Until last night?" An uncomfortable feeling was beginning to grow in Jane's breast. Unthinkingly, she pulled the sheet up to hide her nakedness.

Stephen leaned forward to kiss her on the mouth. "This weekend hasn't been boring for me. It's been the fulfillment of a dream. You were always my dream girl, Janie. But this weekend I got to live out some of my dreams. You are my Caitlin. I wrote that opera about you. How could you not know it?"

CHAPTER EIGHT

Why am I so disturbed? Jane asked herself as Stephen bundled her into his station wagon. It wasn't as if she hadn't suspected that when they'd been undergraduates he'd cherished some sort of adolescent crush on her. Maybe she'd never admitted it to herself, but some part of her had known.

His revelation about *Caitlin* had come as a shock. Yet even that wasn't a total surprise. Hadn't she been uncomfortable about the character Caitlin from the start? Deep down she'd suspected that there was some connection in Stephen's mind between herself and the elusive dream goddess who was the centerpiece of his opera.

Yet it was one thing to harbor unformulated suspicions and quite another to hear them baldly confirmed.

The car's tires protested in the snow, and then the four-wheel drive took hold and Stephen backed out into the road. "What did I tell you?" he said cheerfully. "I'll have you back home in a jiffy."

Jane shivered inside her jacket. It wasn't really from the cold. There was a frigid feeling in her stomach that had nothing to do with the outside temperature. She knew what this weekend had meant to her. When she'd walked into Stephen's house she'd been damaged goods. She was leaving whole, confident that all along she'd only needed the right man and that at last she'd found him. But what had it meant to Stephen? Was he sitting beside her feeling triumphant because he'd finally bedded his teenage fantasy? For him had it all been just a way to get over a youthful hangup?

The car left the lake road and headed out onto the country lane that connected with the highway. The snowplows had been through, so it was easier driving. "We'll be at your place in ten minutes," Stephen commented.

Jane turned her gaze from the window and fixed it on his profile. "And then what?"

He shot her a glance. "What do you mean?"

"Now that you've finally managed to maneuver your Caitlin surrogate into bed, where do we go from here?"

The cynical words, along with the slightly shrill edge of her voice, shocked him. Abruptly he turned the wheel, pulled the car over to the side of the deserted road, and killed the engine. "What the hell did you mean by a remark like that?"

"I mean, what now?"

"We go on seeing each other, of course! How could you think anything else?"

Jane needed to say what was on her mind. "Stephen, if I really understood what you told me back at your cottage, you've been walking around for ten years remembering me as some sort of goddess. But I'm no superhuman. I'm a very real flesh and blood person with problems. I catch colds. Sometimes I feel grouchy. Sometimes I make a mess of things. I can't live up to your goddess image. I don't even want to try."

Without speaking, he reached over her and flipped a lever. Jane's seat went back and all at once she found herself lying flat with Stephen hovering over her. His hands were spread on either side of her shoulders, his face only inches away. "That's nonsense and you know it," he ground out. "You don't have to do anything to live up to my image of you. Janie, you only have to be yourself."

"I'm beginning to wonder if I am a real person to you." She met his gaze squarely. "Are you so fixated on memories and fantasies that when you really do get to know me you'll be disillusioned?"

His face darkened. "I'm already learning what a little fool you can be. Don't say another dumb word." Then he kissed her, his lips peremptorily silencing any further protest. Jane tried to hold herself aloof. But it wasn't possible. Stephen's nose and cheeks against hers were cool from the frigid air, a sharp contrast to the furnacelike heat of his mouth. At first its pressure was hard, letting her know who was in charge. But when he felt the beginnings of her response, he softened and began to tease. His lips moved to each side of hers, nibbling on their sensitive corners, and finally he darted his tongue deep inside her mouth in a playful, erotic mimicry of the act of love.

Jane adored the feeling of his skin and mouth on hers. Though she knew she should resent it, she liked his possessiveness and masculine aggression. It was flattering to be reassured in this way, and she was glad that he wasn't going to listen to any more objections about continuing their relationship. She couldn't hold back for long, and with a faint moan gave in altogether, meeting his tongue with hers and kissing him back ardently.

At last, when there was no question about her capitulation, he propped himself on his elbows and looked down at her, his eyes crinkling at the corners. "How can I become disillusioned by getting to know you if you won't give me the chance?"

She stared up at him, breathless, unable to answer.

"Well," he prodded, "are you going to give me the chance?"

"To become disillusioned?"

"To be even crazier about you than I already am."

"Yes."

Satisfied, he kissed the tip of her nose and then helped her back up into a sitting position. "Good. We'll start on the project just as soon as we get back to your place." Jane felt something tighten deep inside her stomach. She knew what that meant. Soon they would be making love again. And, Lord help her, there was no way she could refuse either of them that pleasure.

Though the weather during the next couple of weeks stayed cold, it was spring as far as Jane was concerned. She saw Stephen almost every day. They spent Saturday and Sunday together at his place. But often during the week he would drive her home from rehearsals and stay for dinner. Afterward they would go into Jane's tiny living room and linger over a glass of wine.

They didn't always make love. Sometimes they would just talk, Stephen stretching out on the sofa with his head in her lap while she twined his dark curls around her fingers. But more often he would pull her face down to his, their lips would meet, and within brief minutes their bodies would be twisted together in the sweetest communion of all.

During this precious time Jane was happier than she ever remembered being before in her life. But the sunny emotion wasn't entirely unshadowed. Past experience had taught her to be wary of happiness. Wasn't there always a fly in the ointment somewhere? And, unfortunately, with Stephen she already knew what it was. Since *Caitlin* was to be performed early in February, he'd stepped up the rehearsal schedule. Jane practiced for the title role almost every night, and each time she sang the words he'd written she was reminded that Caitlin was really her own ghost, Stephen's romanticized memory of the Janie he'd known when he was nineteen.

How could you live up to an image that for ten years had been wrapped in dreams? Jane asked herself. Sometimes, when she dressed with special care for Stephen and went to extra lengths to fix his favorite food, she wondered if she wasn't really putting on an act. Was she hiding her real self with all its flaws and pretending to embody the perfect dream woman of his imaginings? And if that was so, what would happen when he found out that she was only a masquerader, just an ordinary woman and not the peerless female he imagined her to be at all?

She was so troubled by the question that one afternoon she had an oblique discussion about it with Carlie. The two young women were enjoying a cup of coffee together at the Student Union cafeteria. Though Jane and Stephen had tried to be discreet about their blossoming relationship, it hadn't escaped the department secretary's eagle eye.

"I'd ask you to baby-sit Davy this Saturday," she said slyly, "but I suspect you have other plans. You and Dreamboat Hammond are really seeing a lot of each other, aren't you?"

"Yes," Jane admitted, wondering who else had

noticed and whether she should start worrying about her reputation.

The brunette scrutinized her with bright eyes. "I'm not going to ask you whether or not it's serious. I can tell by the way he looks at you that he thinks you wear a halo around your head."

The remark disturbed Jane more than Carlie could appreciate. She looked down into her coffee cup. "Stephen and I knew each other ten years ago, and sometimes I wonder if he hasn't got me mixed up with the girl he thought I was then."

Carlie looked puzzled.

"I mean . . ." Jane struggled for words and then let her voice trail off. How could she explain the complicated relationship between her and Stephen? And why was she even trying? Much as she liked Carlie, the last thing she wanted to do was air her personal problems with the gossipy department secretary.

But Carlie began her own interpretation. "Maybe I know what you mean. Sometimes I think that living together is a surefire way of killing romance. When a man and woman are with each other on a day-to-day basis, struggling to make ends meet—it's a far cry from moonlight and roses." She sighed. "I wonder if that wasn't what went wrong between Bill and me," she remarked, referring to her ex-husband. "When it came to harsh reality, our love for each other just wasn't strong enough. So he turned to someone else."

Jane was quick to offer her sympathy, and the discussion veered off to the history of Carlie's marital difficulties. It was the first time Jane had heard the whole story, and because it was obvious that Carlie needed to talk, she did her best to be a good listener.

Later that evening, Jane sat alone in her tiny living room comparing her friend's tale of woe with her own. There were a number of parallels. Both women had ex-husbands with wandering eyes. And in both cases the marriage had failed because of the difference between fantasy and reality. Carlie claimed that marriage had destroyed the romance between her and her ex. Jane thought that in her own case the situation was more complicated, yet curiously the same. It wasn't just a matter of losing the romance. The problems had been more deep-seated than that. From the start her ill-fated union with Ward had been based on illusion—his about her and hers about marriage. The reality of day-to-day living had quickly turned those illusions into a mockery.

And what about herself and Stephen? Jane wondered. Wasn't his passion for her the product of an illusion? She stood up and began to pace back and forth, a feeling of terror gripping her. Then she stopped and took several deep breaths. It was silly to think this way. So Stephen was enamored of a make-believe heroine for which she was merely the look-alike. Sure, that probably wouldn't stand up to a heavy dose of reality, but it wasn't as if they were going to live together or be married. After his opera was performed he would go back to his old life in Hollywood and they wouldn't see each other. What was happening between them was an affair, not a lifetime commitment. Surely she deserved this brief happiness, she told herself. What did it matter that it was built on sand?

During this period Jane's satisfying new love life wasn't the only thing she had to crow about. Two weeks before Christmas her choral music class's production of *The Messiah* went off beautifully. After the performance Professor Hunt stopped by her office to offer his congratulations. "I'm very impressed by what you've managed to accomplish in your short time here," he told her. "I want you to know that barring some unforeseen circumstance, your appointment will be renewed next year."

His words made Jane feel as bubbly as a freshly opened bottle of champagne. For the first time in her life she'd made a place for herself, and she'd done it all on her own. The realization filled her with such a profound mixture of pride and happiness that for many minutes after Professor Hunt left her office, she sat at her desk with tears in her eyes, seeing nothing but grinning from ear to ear.

She didn't really come back down to earth until that night. Stephen had stopped by for dinner. Afterward, as they washed the dishes together and tidied up her kitchen, he told her that he had to fly back to California over the weekend.

"There's a movie deal in the works and I need to be there for the final discussions," he explained as he removed the plug in the sink and let all the soapy water drain out.

"What kind of a movie?"

"It's a Western, believe it or not. But they want an original score, something memorable and different. I think it might be a nice change of pace for me." He turned toward her and propped himself against the edge of the counter. Along with his favorite faded jeans, he was wearing the ridiculous Minnie Mouse sweatshirt again.

"How long will you be gone?"

"I'll be back late Sunday night." He pushed back a dark curl and looked at her speculatively. "Why don't you come with me?"

Jane was startled. "Why? I'd only be in the way."

"No you wouldn't. We could stay at my beach house. I'd be gone during the day, but you could lie out on the sand and catch some sun. Wouldn't that be a nice change from the snow and freezing temperatures around here?"

Jane had to admit that it would, and Stephen, now that he'd gotten hold of the idea, pursued it enthusiastically.

"Marsh Hughes, one of the producers, is throwing a big party Saturday night. It will be your chance to get a look at a sinful Hollywood bash. Come on, say you'll go! It'll be fun!"

Jane had her doubts, but one by one Stephen rolled over them. She was beginning to understand why he always succeeded at whatever he tried. He might seem like a good-humored, easygoing tease, but when he wanted something he had the tenacity of a snapping turtle. His jaws locked and he wouldn't let go.

"Stephen, I can't afford a ticket to California," she finally protested.

"You'll be my guest. I'll pay your way."

"I can't accept that."

"Why not?" He stepped close and spanned her trim waist with his hands. "Jane, please, I want you with me. I want you to see what the other part of my life is like. And I think it will be good for us to spend some time together away."

Maybe he was right, she thought. Here at Skyler she was getting a very narrow view of the man with whom she'd fallen so hopelessly in love. Maybe it was time for her to see him in his natural habitat and give herself a chance of understanding his way of living a little better. "All right," she agreed. But even as she said the words she had a feeling she was going to regret them.

Jane worried over her wardrobe for the trip. What did people wear to Hollywood parties? she wondered as she eyed the meager supply of garments in her closet. On her small salary she couldn't afford any trendy new clothes, and the only thing like a cocktail dress she had was of pale blue silk and cut on simple lines. It was left over from her days as the shy and frightened wife of a Boston lawyer. The dress was an expensive one that Ward had selected. He'd had excellent if rather subdued taste, and she knew it looked good on her. But would it do for a tinsel-town bash?

When Stephen drove her to the airport Friday afternoon, he was wearing jeans and his old corduroy jacket and carrying no luggage.

"Don't you need to take some clothes?" Jane inquired.

"I have a closet full of stuff at home."

"Will your house be all right? I mean, it's been closed up for three months."

"My cleaning service has been coming in once a week. They'll have the place ready for us when we get there." He dazzled her with his flashing grin. "I can't wait to show it to you. I bet you'll love the view."

Hours later, when they reached the West Coast and a taxi let them off in front of an ultramodern redwood and glass structure perched high on stilts above the sand, Jane was stunned. The house was as beautiful as Stephen had promised. It looked right out on the ocean, and Jane could see the tide was coming in. It seemed to her that at any moment the entire house could be washed out to sea.

When she told Stephen her fears he only chuckled and draped an affectionate arm over her shoulders. "Don't worry. It's well-anchored. After the tide is in all the way, the house is completely surrounded by water. It's almost like being on a ship." He favored her with a mock leer. "Now that I've managed to lure you here, I can pretend I'm a pirate captain who's just captured a fair maiden. See, there's even a plank," he pointed out as they walked over a sort of drawbridge that arched over the water that was beginning to swirl across the sand. The wooden walkway led onto the porch, which was wrapped around the house like a low-slung belt.

It was obvious to Jane that Stephen was delighted to be back home. As he opened the door and ushered her inside, he smiled broadly. Once over the threshold, Jane stood staring around. The bottom floor was nothing but a big living area with a small open kitchen at one end. Everything sparkled, indicating that someone must have been around to clean within the last few hours. But it wouldn't be hard to keep this house tidy, Jane speculated, since there was almost nothing in it. Only a few pieces of comfortable-looking leather furniture and a couple of handwoven Indian rugs brightened the expanse of polished teak floor and the natural cypress walls. At the opposite end from the door there was a handsome grand piano with antique hand-turned legs. Next to it a bank of electronic equipment, including a synthesizer and complicated-looking recording gear, occupied floor space.

But that wasn't what made Jane's eyes widen. It was the windows. Three sides of the house were almost entirely glass, giving the huge living space an airy feeling—as if it were floating somewhere between sea and sky. Though Skyler was a pretty place to live, it had nothing to match this.

"It's really wonderful," Jane murmured as she walked farther into the room.

Stephen sounded pleased and proud. "I'm glad you like it. I always wanted to live in a houseboat or on a low-flying cloud, so I spent a lot of time working with the architect on this design. Sunsets and sunrises are spectacular around here, and the house is angled so you can catch both."

"I'll bet they're really something." Jane crossed to one of the windows and studied the horizon. The sun was already beginning to lower, so it wouldn't be long before she saw for herself. She remembered then that Stephen had described composing one of Caitlin's arias during a sunrise. Now she could picture how it must have been. She turned and gave Stephen a bright smile. "I'm on Eastern time and it's long past my dinner hour. What are we going to do about food?"

"Eat here." He strode toward the kitchen. "I arranged for my housekeeper to buy out a grocery store and cram it into the refrigerator. What would you say to steak, French bread, and a tomato salad?"

"I'd say *voilà!*"

They ate their dinner on the porch next to the sea, and when their meal was finished they sat for a long time talking quietly, admiring the stars and holding each other's hand. Later they went upstairs to the loft, which overlooked the living room, and made silent but strangely intense love. When it was over Stephen drifted off to sleep almost right away. But it was a long time before Jane closed her eyes. And she awoke early enough to tiptoe downstairs alone and see for herself the sunrise in which her lover had composed music for Caitlin. It was every bit as spectacular as she'd imagined and certainly provided the proper ambience for the birth of a goddess.

When Stephen found Jane she was sitting on the porch with a lost expression on her face. He sensed that something was wrong, that something was troubling her. But he couldn't put his finger on what it might be, and since he'd gotten up later than he'd intended, there was no time to find out.

"I'm sorry I'm going to have to leave you here alone all day," he apologized.

"Do you have to go right away? Can't you have a cup of coffee with me first?"

He glanced at his watch and frowned. "No. The appointment was for eight, and they'll have breakfast waiting for me there. Frankly, I'm anxious to get the ball rolling on this thing." He dropped a kiss on her forehead and massaged her shoulder gently. "Are you sure you wouldn't like to come along and tour the studio?"

She shook her head. "No, I'll just soak up some sun. I've never had a beach all to myself before."

Stephen gazed down at her thoughtfully. He had the nagging feeling that something was wrong and that he shouldn't leave her. "Janie, maybe I should cancel—"

But she only laughed at him. "Don't be ridiculous. You didn't fly all the way out here not to go to this thing. I'll be fine." Then she aimed him at the door and gave him a playful little shove.

When he was gone she went upstairs to change her clothes. Inadvertently, she opened the wrong drawer and discovered a collection of Stephen's T-shirts. The first one she picked up read, "True connoisseur of cheap wine and sleazy women." Shaking her head and smiling, she put it away. Then she donned her bathing suit, grabbed a half-finished mystery novel she'd brought along, and went outside to lie on the sand. It really was a beautiful place, she told herself. The tide was out and the private beach seemed to stretch endlessly, its golden surface undulating gently in the sunshine.

But it wasn't long before Jane's winter-white skin had received more than its share of sun, and she had to retreat to the shelter of the house. There she puttered around for the rest of the morning, trying out Stephen's beautiful piano and listening to some of the tapes in his enormous collection. For lunch she fixed herself a salad and sat out on the deck. Between forksful of lettuce and cottage cheese, she stared out at the sea, which was once more beginning to roll in beneath the house. As she listened to the soft sighing sound it made as it crept over the sand, she wondered why she felt so depressed.

This reminds me of something, she thought. Then she realized what. It was like the long empty days she'd spent in Boston. While she'd tried to find ways to pass the time by doing meaningless things in their lonely apartment, Ward had been out wheeling and dealing, making his mark on the world—and finding a woman who suited him better.

Of course it was ridiculous to compare that time with this. She was here for only a couple of days, on vacation, really. Stephen was a man with whom she was having a temporary affair, not a husband who was bored with her and had locked her away so that she wouldn't interfere with his "real" life. Nevertheless, it felt the same. *I should have gone with Stephen to the studio,* she thought. But it was too late now. She was marooned for the rest of the long afternoon.

When Stephen finally got back it was dark and Jane had long ago fixed herself a light dinner and eaten alone. As he walked in the door he looked tired but elated.

"Sorry I'm so late. How's your day been?"

"Fine," Jane lied. "How about yours?"

"Great! I think this deal is just about sewed up." He glanced at his watch. "Marsh's house is a long drive from here. We should probably get started in an hour or so. I'm going to take a quick shower."

As he took the steps to the loft two at a time, Jane stared after him. Where was the easygoing guy she'd known from Skyler? The hard-driving, energetic Stephen she was catching a glimpse of here in California was a new experience. Was he like this all the time when he was on his own stamping ground?

Upstairs, as hot water sluiced down over his body, Stephen felt jubilant. Closing a deal on a new project was always exciting. But the true morale booster was being here with Jane. It was a real high to bring her to this house where he'd spent so many nostalgic nights remembering her and thinking she was lost to him forever. He couldn't even begin to explain what it had meant to him to make love to her last night with the sound of his own private stretch of sea whispering around them. Now he would be able to show her off to his friends. It was going to make him feel so proud!

On the long ride to Beverly Hills, Stephen carried on a largely one-sided conversation. Jane kept glancing sideways at him, feeling almost as if she were with a stranger. It wasn't just the flame-red Maserati he was driving down the highway like a rocket to the moon. It was the way he looked.

She'd never seen him dressed up before. Now, over a white silk shirt open at the throat, he was wearing a black suit that had obviously been cut by a master tailor. Sometime today he'd gotten a haircut. For the first time since she'd known him, his curls were under control. He looked like a different person—suave, sophisticated, purposeful, and, yes, dangerous.

"What happened to your hair?" she asked.

"Oh, André had a few spare minutes so he had a go at me with his scissors. He does all the studio's heartthrobs."

"Well, he's very good at his job. You look wonderful."

"Thanks. So do you—as always." He reached over and patted her knee.

Jane glanced down at the skirt of her blue silk dress and wished she'd shopped for something different. Next to this new Stephen she felt dowdy. The feeling mushroomed when they arrived at Marsh Hughes's mansion.

Stephen parked his sports car amid a gaggle of Mercedes, Porsches, Cadillacs, and Rolls-Royces and then walked her to huge carved double doors. To her right Jane glimpsed an enormous pool strung with lights and occupied by nymphets in bikinis so brief they might as well be naked. To one side there was a set of tennis courts, and on all the sides she could see the property commanded a breathtaking view of the surrounding hills. From inside the house there was a dull roar of merriment. When a servant opened the doors and admitted Jane and Stephen, the roar became a deafening explosion. Jane had felt uncertain about this party; suddenly the emotion she experienced was closer to panic.

The noise didn't seem to faze her roguishly handsome escort. With his hand around Jane's wrist and his dark eyes sparkling with anticipation, he threaded his way through the crowd until he found their host. Marsh Hughes was a heavyset blond man with an air of cynical amusement. He gave Jane an approving look, winked at Stephen, and whispered, "I've always liked the Princess Grace type myself. Junie is over at the bar," he added, pointing out a plump blond woman in a low-cut gown who Jane later discovered was his wife. "Make yourselves at home, you two." He touched Stephen's shoulders. "Hammond, I'd like to get together with you for another little talk later on, but for now, enjoy."

Jane wondered how she was going to enjoy herself in this crowd of raucous strangers. She looked around at the other guests. All the women seemed incredibly beautiful, with masses of hair in unlikely colors and makeup so artful and sometimes so fanciful Jane simply had to stop and stare. They were dressed either in glittering designer gowns or costumes that ranged from fringed Indian dresses to white satin decorated with ostrich feathers. Next to them her own conservatively cut dress looked absurdly out of place. She would have been better off coming in jeans and a silk blouse.

Feeling like a drab tabby cat in a room full of prize-winning Persians, she allowed Stephen to get her a glass of champagne and then lead her around introducing her first to their hostess and then to his friends. Though she tried, it was impossible to remember all their names. Some were famous while others she'd never heard of because they worked with the technical end of movie production. But they all seemed terribly bright and witty and terribly sure of themselves. Just as she'd imagined he would, Stephen fit right in. He was every bit as comfortable in this crowd as he'd been with the worshipful students at Skyler.

"Stevie, darling!" a piercing female voice cried out. Then a strikingly attractive redhead wearing a tight, floor-length dress covered with green sequins pushed her way through the throng milling around in the enormous living room. "Where have you been hiding yourself, for God sake?"

Stephen's face lit. "Hello, Millicent. I've been in Vermont. You know, I told you I was going to take a sabbatical."

The redhead made a little moue. "But it's so cold in Vermont. And I've missed you."

Chuckling, Stephen put his arm around Jane's shoulder. "Jane, let me introduce you to Millicent Proctor. She's a designer at Colossal, and a great friend of mine."

Tearing her gaze away from Stephen's darkly handsome person, the redhead looked Jane up and down, her comprehensive green gaze taking in the neatly chignoned blond hair, the fresh face wearing only a minimum of makeup, the prim and proper blue dress. She didn't comment, but then she didn't have to. Jane knew exactly what the woman was thinking. *She's telling herself that "Stevie" is amusing himself with New England's answer to Alice in Wonderland,* Jane thought grimly.

After a polite greeting, Millicent turned back to Stephen. "Just about everyone's here. Have you seen Margie?"

"Margie Crowell?"

"Margie Norris, silly. She and Crowell split a few months back. Didn't you know?"

"No," Stephen admitted. "I hadn't heard that."

Jane's backbone prickled. Wasn't Margie the name of the woman with whom Stephen had lived? Was this the same Margie? If so, what would that mean to Stephen? she wondered.

For the next hour he stayed close by Jane's side, introducing her to scores of people and carrying on conversations that were to her literally incomprehensible. It seemed as if everyone in the film industry lived in their own private world and spoke their own special language. What was axial illumination? A propriety fractal package?

Why do I feel as if this is something that's happened to me before? Jane wondered as she shifted her weight on feet that were beginning to hurt. She knew she'd never been to a Hollywood party, but the sense of déjà vu was overwhelming. Then she realized why. This was like the affairs in Boston she'd attended with Ward. Oh, the people dressed and acted differently and the conversation was about movies not Boston politics, court cases, and the Arts Council. But her position was the same. She was a naive outsider, tolerated only because of the man she was with. She had nothing to say to these people, and they most certainly had nothing to say to her.

Jane felt itchy inside her dress and her temples were beginning to throb. But somehow she managed to keep a smile pasted on her face. She sensed that this social affair was important to Stephen, and she wasn't going to do anything that might spoil it for him. Close to midnight, their host strolled over and tapped Stephen on the shoulder.

"I've been talking with J. T., Hammond. I think we're about to wrap this thing up. But before we make the final decision on the time frame, we'd both like a few more words with you in private."

Stephen nodded and then turned to Jane. "You'll be okay by yourself for a little while, won't you? This shouldn't take long."

"Of course," she told him. But when he'd strolled off with Marsh and disappeared into the crowd, she felt lost. *What's wrong with me?* she wondered. *I'm a big, grown-up girl. I've been to parties by myself before. It's as if I'm going through some sort of emotional time warp and reverting to the unsure person I was ten years ago.*

Nevertheless, her instinct was to escape, and after picking up a canapé, she threaded her way through knots of chattering people and went outside. Though there were quite a few guests swimming in the pool and milling around its edge, several lawn chairs were unoccupied. Jane dragged one into the shadows and sat down with a sigh of relief. Several minutes later she was joined by a handsome young man wearing tight pants and a black silk shirt open to the navel. He was smoking an acrid-smelling cigarette.

"Want a drag?" he asked as he settled himself in the chair next to her.

"No thanks. I don't smoke."

He narrowed slightly unfocused eyes. "This isn't a regular cigarette, for God's sake. It's a joint."

"I don't smoke joints, either." Well that was one difference from the Boston parties to which Ward had squired her, Jane thought wryly. No one there had ever offered her pot.

Excusing herself, she got up and went back into the house. Maybe by now Stephen was done talking to Marsh Hughes and the mysterious J.T., and she could suggest that they go home. After wandering around for almost twenty minutes she finally spotted her escort. He was out on one of the many decks that led to the elaborately landscaped grounds surrounding the house. He wasn't alone, but deep in conversation with a very attractive woman with streaked shoulder-length blond hair. Their conversation looked so earnest and somehow private that Jane hovered near a velvet drape, reluctant to intrude.

Just then Junie Hughes bustled past. She caught

Jane's eye. "Oh there you are. Having a good time?"

"Fine. It's a lovely party."

"Looking for Stephen? Well, there he is out on the porch talking with Margie Norris," Mrs. Hughes said. She smiled brightly before sailing past.

Jane drew back and then turned away. There was no reason to be upset because Stephen was talking to his old lover. Yet, suddenly, she felt so depressed she wanted to cry. Refusing to give way to the ridiculous impulse, she forced herself to circulate. Picking up a champagne glass and sipping at it from time to time, she walked up to groups of people and stood on their fringes listening to mystifying snatches of conversation. As the evening wore on she even met a few Hollywoodites who seemed both nice and interesting. She was talking with one, an attractive young special-effects man, when Stephen finally found her. "I've been looking for you," he said, draping a possessive arm around her shoulder. "Sorry to have left you alone so long."

"Oh, that's okay," Jane returned airily. "I've been learning the most fascinating things from Jerry here."

After introductions were made and all three exchanged a few words, Jerry drifted off and Jane and Stephen were alone.

"How are you doing?" he asked.

"All right, I guess. A little tired, maybe."

He gave her a concerned look and then glanced at his watch. "It's almost two in the morning, and we're both still on East Coast time. Maybe we should make our excuses and head back."

Jane certainly wasn't going to argue with that. A few minutes later she and Stephen departed.

"Well," he commented as he maneuvered the

Maserati out onto the road, "tomorrow at this time we'll be back in Vermont. Will you be glad to get home?"

"Yes," Jane said. Though he shot her a curious look, she didn't expand on that. Time enough to tell him what was really in her mind when they arrived in Skyler. Meanwhile, she had a lot of thinking to do—a lot of very painful thinking.

CHAPTER NINE

"You've been awfully quiet." Stephen's station wagon crunched up the gravel drive to Jane's apartment and then rolled to a stop. It was after midnight and the houses on the street were dark. An icy wind blew, which was a shock after California's sunny climate. "You fell asleep in the car last night, and I don't believe that you've said more than a dozen words to me since we left the airport."

"I'm tired," Jane hedged. Then she shifted—maybe now was the time to tell Stephen what was in her mind. Since she'd been behaving like a zombie ever since that party, he must know that something was wrong. "I've been doing a lot of thinking."

"About what?"

"About us."

Stephen aimed a sharp look in her direction. "Nothing that's going to shock me, I hope." When she didn't respond he switched off the engine and said quietly, "What's on your mind?"

Jane didn't want to discuss this in the car. "How about coming in for a cup of coffee?"

"I thought you'd never ask." He got out to open the door for her, but by the time he'd walked around the car, she was already standing in the drive. After removing her small suitcase from the back Stephen followed her up the stairs. When they were inside he demanded, "What's going on, Janie?"

She flipped on a light and went into the kitchen. "I'll have coffee ready in a jiffy."

He followed her. "What's wrong?" All day she'd been acting strangely, treating him with the distant politeness one might show a visiting dignitary and staring out the window of the plane as if she were pondering the problems of the universe. Would he ever understand this woman? he wondered. Just when he thought he was on the right track with her, she sidestepped.

Jane stood still, her hands resting lightly on the countertop. She didn't look back at Stephen, but she could feel him watching her. Though his hair still looked too neat, in his corduroy jacket and jeans he was almost back to his old self again. But that didn't matter; she'd seen through his disguise. He was a sophisticate from a world to which she could never belong, and their affair could never be anything but just that—a temporary fling. She'd known that all along and told herself that it was all right, but now she'd come to her senses. "Everything's wrong," she said. "We have to stop seeing each other."

"What?" The question was as sharp as the crack of a rifle. "What the hell are you talking about?"

"I haven't been thinking these past few weeks, but it's time I did." She turned to face him. "I want to call it off."

"My God, why?" He'd never expected anything like this from her. Just the opposite, he'd hoped this trip would bring them closer together. What in hell was going on?

To still her trembling hands, Jane pressed her palms together and tried to explain. "You can't know what I went through to be where I am now. After Ward left me my self-esteem was zero, and I didn't even know how I was going to support myself. But I fought my way back. It took me five years, but I've got a new career and a new life. I can't let that be taken away. I can't be knocked off my pins again."

"Jane, turn around and look at me, dammit! I'm not here to take anything away from you. And as for knocking you off anything, I thought I was part of your new life."

"You are." Jane pivoted so that they were confronting each other, but at the outraged expression on Stephen's face, her gaze wavered and she looked down at her hands. "You helped me. You made me realize there's nothing wrong with me, and I'll always be grateful."

Cursing, he strode forward and took her by the shoulders. "What are you saying?" he exploded. "Surely you don't think that what's passed between us was some kind of therapy?"

She looked up, a hint of defiance in her blue eyes. "It was in a way."

The veins on Stephen's neck stood out sharply and his jaw clenched. "Oh, that's just great! Ole Doc Hammond, your friendly campus sex therapist. Listen, Jane, for me it was nothing of the sort. For me it was lovemaking—with the emphasis on the first syllable."

"You talk about love," she shot back, "but you intend to leave here in a couple of months and go back to your life in Hollywood. Isn't that so?"

Stephen's eyes narrowed. "Janie, did something happen at that party of Marsh's to upset you? Did you by any chance see me talking to Margie Norris and draw some dumb conclusions?"

"I did see you with her."

"I thought it must be something like that!" He shook her gently. "Jane, we're just friends now. I'm not in love with her. I never was."

Jane stared up at him wondering how she could explain her feelings. Margie wasn't the issue, though it had been disturbing to see him with her. It had underlined the "otherness" of his life, the fact that they were really worlds apart.

"You haven't answered my question," she finally whispered. "When your opera is produced you're going back to California, aren't you?"

He couldn't deny it. "Yes."

"Where does that leave me?"

"You could come with me. That's what this trip was all about in a way—to show you what your options were."

"Well, it did that." Stepping sideways, she shook herself free of his grasp. For the past weeks she'd been like a blind person, leaving herself open to all kinds of hurt. Not only was Stephen's life totally alien to hers, he was in love with a dream. Sooner or later he would realize that that dream had no substance. In the meantime, she was a real human being building a life of her own, and now she had to be sensible and protect herself from her own weaknesses. "Stephen," she said as gently as she could, "Hollywood isn't for me. I don't want anything to do with it."

He stared, stunned and not quite believing what was happening. Where was the warm and giving lover who'd lain in his arms? He hardly recognized the cold woman who stood before him.

"I can't believe this. You're telling me that you don't want any part of my life?"

Jane gathered her fears around her like a mantle

and held them close. It was horrible to hear herself saying these things to the man she loved, but in the long run maybe it was better to make a clean break. Dragging things out would only make them worse.

"Yes, I guess I am telling you that. You're going to leave, but I have to stay here. It's better to recognize that fact and not make it any worse for ourselves than it already is. It's better to stop this before either of us gets in any deeper."

For a full minute, Stephen continued to regard her. Jane felt as if she were shrinking under his steady gaze, but she refused to back down. She already felt shattered. If they stayed lovers, she would be an emotional basket case by the time he left. And what if she weakened and went back with him to Hollywood? She'd be giving up everything she'd worked so hard to build here in order to put herself in the same sort of position she'd been in with Ward. No, it was unthinkable!

"Jane, we're already in so deep that we're both drowning," he finally said. "You're tired. I'm going to leave you now. But this discussion isn't over. I'll call you tomorrow."

He could dial the phone all he wanted, Jane thought as she watched him turn toward the door. She wouldn't answer. The discussion was over, and so was their affair.

True to his word, Stephen did call. Persistently, her phone rang. And when it wasn't ringing he was knocking on her front door demanding that they "talk." Finally, in her fearful desperation, Jane resorted to something that made her ashamed of herself.

"Stephen," she told him when she opened her door a few mornings after their return from California to find him waiting on her porch, "if you don't stop this, I'm going to resign my role in *Caitlin.*"

Stephen's face was already pinched from the cold, but now it went even whiter. "You can't mean that. The performance is only four weeks off."

"I do mean it." It wasn't true. She would never do that to him. But he had no way of knowing that her threat was an empty one. He said nothing—only turned and walked back down the steps to his car. And as Jane watched him go she felt like putting her face in her hands and sobbing. But she couldn't give him any more opportunities to get past her defenses. It was, she told herself, just a matter of holding on until *Caitlin* was performed. Then he would return to his old life and she would be left in peace to try and pull together the raveled threads of hers.

But it wasn't so simple. After her threat, Stephen gave up calling. But they still saw each other at rehearsals.

"You're not standing right," he shouted late one afternoon the week before Christmas. "When Caitlin sings that aria she's feeling joyful and triumphant. You look about as triumphant as a wet rag doll. Do something different with your arms."

"Like what?" Jane gritted, glaring at the spot where he sat in the darkened auditorium. Since their breakup Stephen had seemed to be dissatisfied with everything she did, and she was close to the end of her rope.

"Here, I'll show you." He jumped up onto the stage and crossed toward her. Today he was wearing a gray sweatshirt with black letters that read, "I am an Unidentified Flying Object." When he stood no more than a foot from her and grasped her wrist, Jane stubbornly fixed her gaze on the word "Unidentified." He might be a UFO, she thought, but there was certainly no big mystery about what he was doing. He was trying to get under her skin.

"Your arms should be up, like this," he told her as he began to arrange her body to his liking.

Jane fought to still her trembling reaction. There were half a dozen interested students watching. Even so, Stephen's hands on her arms were like a caress, and she knew that during rehearsals he was deliberately finding excuses to touch her. "When are you going to stop this sort of thing?" she muttered through her teeth.

"When are you going to quit behaving like such a little fool?" he retorted under his breath. Then, in a more persuasive tone of voice, he added, "For God's sake, Jane, let me drive you home tonight. We need a chance to talk in private."

"No."

As if he were positioning a ballet dancer, he began to adjust the fingers on her right hand. His thumb slipped into the sensitive center of her palm and moved in small circular motions. "What you're doing doesn't make any sense. It's Christmas next week. We're both going to be miserable if we don't spend it together."

Refusing to meet his eyes, Jane stepped back and cleared her throat. "All right, Mr. Hammond," she said in a loud voice. "I think I know what to do with my arms now. Shall we run through the number again?"

Stephen's dark gaze expressed the many words that he couldn't speak aloud. Then he shrugged. "All right, let's do that."

As it turned out, Christmas was not as bad as Jane had feared. In desperation she accepted Carlie's invitation to spend the holiday with her family. After a sumptuous dinner Carlie's parents disappeared into the back room to watch television while the two young women washed up. When they were done they went out into the living room to watch Davy play with his toys under the tree. Jane had given him a truck he could take apart and "fix."

"You certainly made a hit with that," Carlie commented.

Jane grinned. "It's more fun giving him presents than it is to get them yourself."

"There's nothing like a kid at Christmas," Carlie agreed.

Her casual words sent a little stab of pain through Jane. What if she and Stephen had stayed together long enough to have children? She pictured a dark-eyed little boy with a wreath of onyx curls. The image was painfully vivid. Pushing it away as though it were an assailant, she turned to Carlie. "I'm awfully glad I didn't stay home by myself." On this particular day anything was better than being alone with her thoughts.

"Bill is alone," Carlie commented. "That affair he had didn't last, and the woman is with someone else now. He wanted to spend Christmas with Davy and me, but I knew my parents wouldn't like it if he came over. They still resent what happened between us."

Jane studied her friend curiously. "Are you seeing much of your ex-husband these days?"

Carlie leaned forward and lowered her voice. "I haven't mentioned it to my folks yet, but I have to tell someone. I think that Bill and I are going to get back together."

Jane cocked her head. "That's a surprise. I thought you never wanted to have anything more to do with him."

"That's what I thought too." Carlie sighed. "But never is a long time. I've been lonely and I've missed him. I still love Bill, and now I think that when you love someone you have to try everything you can to make things work—even if that involves forgetting your pride and making some compromises. This time that's what I intend to do."

"What do you mean?"

Carlie's dark eyes were deeply serious. "I mean that I want this man enough to change my way of doing some things and to try and fit my life to his."

"But all the changes shouldn't be on your side," Jane objected.

"They're not going to be. Bill and I have talked it all out. He wants to make things work too. And honestly, this time I think we have a shot."

Jane took her friend's hand. "I hope so, I really do."

As Jane walked back to her apartment later that evening, it was impossible for her not to dwell on Carlie's words. She wished the other young woman well in her valiant attempt to patch up her failed marriage. But that wasn't what was really on her mind now. She was thinking about her relationship with Stephen. She'd known that breaking things off with him would be hard, but she hadn't guessed it would be as painful as this. Her nights were sleepless, and getting through her days was like wading through peanut butter. She ached whenever she thought of him—which was all the time. Seeing him at rehearsals was torture. *Another month and it will all be over,* she told herself yet again as she trudged up the stairs toward her front door. *He'll have gone back to California, and I'll be able to pick up the pieces.*

Listlessly, she pulled open the screen. A small package that had been wedged behind it fell out at her feet. Surprised, Jane picked it up and took it inside. It was wrapped in Christmas paper, but there was no card. Shrugging off her coat, she began to untie the gold ribbon that secured the red printed paper. When she'd uncovered a white box she hesitated before lifting the lid. Somehow she already knew what would be inside. Her stomach felt queasy when she found out that she'd guessed right. The box contained the silver pendant she'd lost ten years earlier. It had been polished, presumably by a jeweler, and its chain had been repaired.

Beneath the square of white cotton on which it rested there was a folded sheet of paper. "I can't keep this any longer," it read. "If I take anything home to California with me next time, it has to be given freely. Love, S."

For a long time Jane stood staring down at the note. It was only when her vision started to be blurred that she put it down and ran into her bedroom, where she flung herself down on her bed and cried in the darkness. There was no way she could go to California. It just wouldn't work. But giving him up hurt terribly. "I just want it to be over," she whispered through her tears. "I just want it to be over!"

On New Year's Eve he called.

"Jane?"

She recognized his voice on the other end of the line instantly. "Yes."

"I'm here alone," he said, "sitting in front of the fire thinking about you. I need to see you. Will you let me come over?"

It was close to midnight, and she guessed that he'd been drinking. There was a slight slur in his voice. "Stephen, no."

"For God's sake!"

"Please!" She put her hand over her heart, which was beating crazily. "It just isn't going to work, and you know it as well as I do."

"Nothing works unless you give it a chance," he shot back. "You're not giving it a chance. And I don't understand why."

"Our life-styles are incompatible."

"That's absurd. If you really believe that, the least you can do is discuss it with me. We're intelligent people, we can work things out. But that isn't really it. There's something else bugging you. Let me come over and talk to you about it."

No, Jane thought, she wasn't going to give him the chance to sweet-talk her. When she'd married Ward she'd given up her career for a man and that had turned out disastrously. She knew that she'd be a fool to do it all over again for Stephen—especially when it wasn't really her he loved. He was enamored of a fantasy woman, not one made of flesh and blood who had all too many flaws.

"No," she said.

"Happy New Year," he said bitterly, and then hung up the phone with a crash.

Jane might have been able to ignore her conviction that Stephen's true love was really a glorified memory if she hadn't been singing the part of Caitlin almost every afternoon. The performance of the opera was scheduled for January fifteenth and rehearsals during the first two weeks of that month reached an even higher emotional pitch. The trouble between Jane and Stephen was part of that. He never spoke to her about his New Year's Eve call, but the painful feelings it had exacerbated crackled in the air between them.

In a desperate attempt to distract herself, Jane accepted a couple of dates with Dan Wilkens. Over the past months she'd grown to like the pleasant young violin teacher. He made a cheerful companion, and his undemanding company was soothing. Seeing a man socially who wasn't Stephen, she told herself, was also a step in the right direction. Though her anguish over their breakup had only increased in intensity, at least she was trying to do something about it.

When the night for the *Caitlin* premiere finally arrived, Jane's nerves were strung so tight that she was afraid of fainting onstage. But she was too much the professional for that. So much depended on the success of the performance. It wasn't just that Stephen's prestige and that of Skyler's music department would be enhanced by a good show. There were the budding young singers who had rehearsed faithfully week after week. If Jane didn't come through, everyone else would be made to look bad too.

All these things were in her mind when the curtain rose for the first act. Though the overflowing audience was a blur and she was only dimly aware of their polite applause, she could clearly see Stephen watching her intently as he raised his baton to start the music for her opening aria. Out of the corner of her eye she caught Alberta giving her the high sign from the wings. Smiling faintly, Jane took a deep breath, closed her eyes, and mentally slipped into the role of Caitlin. She'd come to fear and despise the goddess Stephen had created, but tonight she would use all the skill she possessed to bring her nemesis to life.

Instead of forgetting her lines or quavering on a high note, she sang the part with every ounce of emotion she had. The rest of the cast seemed to catch fire from her impassioned performance, and when the final curtain came down and they all linked hands to take their bows, the applause from the audience was thunderous.

"You were terrific!" Alberta whispered as they left the stage. "You brought tears to my eyes."

"You were terrific too," Jane returned, giving the redhead's hand an encouraging squeeze.

"Oh no, it was all you. If I sang decently, it was just because I had to when you were so perfect. Watching you was like . . . I don't know . . . like a spiritual experience." Alberta's round eyes brimmed with sincerity. "You *were* Caitlin!"

"Oh, not really," Jane returned dryly.

There was to be a cast party after the show, but she felt far too drained to attend it. When she got back to her dressing room she collapsed on the bench in front of the mirror feeling almost too exhausted even to take off her makeup. A few minutes later there was a gentle tap at her door. It was Dan Wilkens.

"Congratulations on a stunning performance!"

Turning, she gave him a weary smile. "Thanks, but right now I feel more stunned than stunning. All I want to do is stagger home so I can fall into bed and sleep for the next forty-eight hours."

Though he smiled his understanding, he also looked concerned. "You shouldn't walk across campus alone in the dark. Let me see you home safely."

She was too strung out to argue, and a few minutes later, after changing into her street clothes, she slipped out a side entrance where he'd arranged to meet her.

"You were fantastic tonight," he complimented her once again. "It was . . . how can I say it right? . . . you *were* Caitlin. It was absolutely electrifying."

"Why, thank you." Jane pulled up the collar on her coat. It was a clear night, but frigid. The stars glittered in the black sky like ice shavings, and already her fingers inside her mittens were stiff with cold.

"I bet Hammond is pleased," Dan went on.

"I wouldn't know. I didn't get a chance to talk to him." In fact, she'd done her best to avoid speaking with Stephen.

"This has got to add a lot of luster to his name. Oh, I know he's big with the movies. But opera is a whole different ball game, and it looks to me as if he's done himself proud with his first effort."

"Yes, I suppose so."

They turned a corner and walked down the street toward Jane's apartment.

"There were a lot of important critics in that audience. Even some of the New York papers were represented," Dan remarked.

"Oh?" Jane knew she wasn't holding up her side of the conversation, but she really couldn't find anything to say. Tomorrow maybe she'd be interested in what the critics wrote, but tonight she was simply too tired.

Finally her companion changed the subject. "I hear Carlie's leaving us next month. Going away with her husband—some sort of reconciliation effort." He shook his head. "The course of true love never did run smooth."

"You can say that again," Jane muttered.

"What?"

She cleared her throat and turned into the drive. "Would you like to come up for a cup of something hot?" She hadn't invited Dan into her apartment before, but she felt guilty about letting him walk her home in the cold, answering all his conversational gambits with monosyllables and then sending him away without even giving him a chance to warm up.

Inside, Jane fixed them each a mug of cocoa. A few minutes later they were sipping it in the living room and talking politely when there was a sharp rap on the door.

Dan gave her an inquiring look. "Were you expecting someone?"

Jane shook her head. Rising to her feet, she went to the door. Stephen stood on the other side, his hands jammed into his pockets. He was still wearing the tuxedo he'd donned for the performance. The only concession he'd made to the cold was a red plaid scarf, which was wound around his neck and carelessly knotted. Frost glittered in his tousled hair and the end of his nose was red. Despite all this, he looked unbearably handsome, and at the sight of him Jane felt her heart constrict.

"Well, surely you're not going to let me stand out here and freeze."

"No." Even if she wanted to, she couldn't turn him away with Dan Wilkens watching. She stepped aside and watched anxiously as Stephen walked in. "Why aren't you at the cast party?"

"Why aren't you?"

"I was too tired."

"Too tired or too gutless?" he said as he strolled past her. He came to a full stop when he spotted her guest. "Well, well." Over his shoulder he shot Jane a look and then turned back to Dan. "How are you doing, Wilkens?"

"Fine," Dan replied affably. "I don't need to ask about you. After that fantastic showcase for your opera, you're probably walking on air."

"Not exactly. You see, I have some important

technical points to go over with my leading lady here." He gestured toward Jane.

Dan's eyebrows began to elevate. "Can't that wait until tomorrow?"

"No it can't. It's imperative to get right on these things while they're fresh in your head, you know." Coolly deliberate, Stephen strode across the room, removed Dan's half-finished cup of cocoa from his fingers, and set it down on the table next to his chair. "So if you don't mind, Wilkens, I'm afraid I'm going to have to send you on your way."

Dan gaped, his gaze swiveling from Stephen's face to Jane's and then back. For a moment it almost looked as if he were going to protest. Then, shrugging, he stood and began pulling on his coat.

At first Jane was too flabbergasted to react at all. Then she rushed forward and picked up the mug of cocoa. "Dan, you don't have to leave."

But he was already heading for the door. "Oh no, don't worry about it," he mumbled. "It's time for me to get home anyhow. I've a lot of papers to grade, you know." And with that he disappeared into the night.

CHAPTER TEN

When Dan was gone Jane turned around and glared at Stephen. "You have no right to throw a guest out of my house! Just what do you think you're doing? Why are you here?"

Coolly, he started to unknot his scarf. "I'm here to talk to you and I don't need an audience. If it hadn't been for your threat to back out of *Caitlin,* I would have pushed my way in here long ago. But now the opera has been performed, so I don't need to worry about that sort of blackmail anymore, do I?" He looked her up and down, his eyes glittering. "It's time we had this out."

"Oh, no!"

"Oh, yes! You didn't really think I was going to let you get away with this, did you, Jane? I'm not some Easter duckling that you can dump in the nearest pond when you get done playing with him. I'm in love with you, and whether or not you're willing to admit it, I think you're in love with me."

She didn't even try to answer because suddenly she had started to tremble. It began with her knees and worked its way up her body so that at last she had to clench her teeth to keep them from chattering.

Apparently unaware of her emotional turmoil, he stepped forward and laid a conciliating hand on her arm. "Jane, you were so wonderful tonight. It was everything I ever dreamed it could be. I couldn't take my eyes off you out on that stage. You *were* Caitlin."

He was the third person she'd heard that from. This time she reacted as if she'd been slapped. The trembling broke out in her hand so uncontrollably that she dropped the cup she'd been holding. The lukewarm cocoa in it sloshed out and onto Stephen's sleeve before puddling on the floor around bits of broken crockery. They both stared down at the cloudy brown liquid.

Jane was the first to speak. "You've got it on your beautiful tuxedo!"

"Forget it. The tuxedo doesn't matter."

But she couldn't take her horrified gaze away from the garment's ruined sleeve. It was as if the stain were an emblem of all the things distressing her these past few weeks. Suddenly her eyes began to burn and tears started to leak from their corners. "Let me try and clean it for you in the kitchen," she whispered.

Stephen stared anxiously at her. "Janie, sweetheart, what's wrong? You're crying, for God's sake. A little spilled cocoa is nothing to cry about."

"It's not that," she said, her voice breaking on the last word.

"Then what is it?" Quickly he shrugged off the jacket and dropped it on the nearest chair. Then he gathered her close and wrapped his arms around her tightly. "Tell me what it is," he whispered against her temple. "Explain it to me, darling. I've been going through hell these past few weeks, so it's time."

But Jane was beyond explanations. Even she didn't understand what was happening. She only knew that it was all too much—the weeks of misery, the strain of tonight's performance, and now Stephen's unexpected appearance, and the wonderful, comforting feel of his strong arms enclosing her. It was more than she could cope with. She began to sob, all her repressed emotions tumbling out in wild disarray.

"Janie, Janie," he said, laying his cheek against the top of her head. "It's going to be all right. I promise."

That only made her cry harder. She wanted so desperately to believe him. But how could it be "all right" when everything was so wrong? Still, she moved closer to him, seeking his warmth as her tears spilled out on his chest. His hard strength felt like a safe harbor. She could hear the steady, reassuring beat of his heart, smell the clean, manly essence of him, feel his lips moving against her hair as he dropped soft kisses into it. She'd missed him so much—his laughter, his touch, his body close to hers.

"Oh, Janie," he groaned. "I've missed you so! Night after night I've lain in bed awake, thinking of you. Do you know what it means to me to hold you in my arms again like this?"

As he spoke his hands stroked her hair and then her back, sensitizing every inch of flesh that he touched. One palm slipped down to the swell of her hip and rested there possessively. Cradled against his pelvis, her breasts pressed into his chest, she felt his other hand tip her face up. Then, as softly as the brush of butterfly wings, his mouth began to travel along her hairline. Trembling, she felt him drop light kisses on her closed eyelids, blotting away the tears that glistened between her lashes.

"Jane, darling, I want you so much. It's been hell

seeing you almost every day and yet not being able to touch you."

It had been hell for her too. Her arms stole around his neck, and she opened her eyes so that she could gaze into the dark beauty of his. Then she pulled his head down and kissed him with all the pent-up longing and fervor that churned inside her. "I want you too," she whispered. "Oh, Stephen, I want you too!"

In one swift motion he picked her up. Cradling her against his chest, he walked out into the hall toward her bedroom. Without bothering to switch on the light, he strode to the bed and laid her on it. Then his taut length covered hers while their mouths met feverishly.

In seconds Jane's clothes seemed to melt from her body, and she felt Stephen's mouth at her breast. Arching toward him, she reveled in the piercing pleasure that coursed through her as he licked and then gently sucked at her stiffened nipples. Her whole body seemed to flame toward his.

"Sweetheart," he groaned, "I can't wait. It's been too long and I've wanted you too much."

"I can't wait either," she whispered back, too caught up in the tide of desire sweeping through her to be shocked by her hoarse admission.

Their lovemaking that night was swift and violent in its frenzied ardor. But when that first passionate burst had softened the edge on their mutual hunger, their encounter took on a different character. While the moonlight filtered through Jane's window they kissed as if each meeting of hands, eyes, mouths held a precious magic.

"You're so beautiful," Stephen told her. "I want to touch you, run my hands over you like this forever."

Jane felt exactly the same. As her fingers drifted over the hard structure of his chest, measured the lean span of his hips, and felt the heat still pulsing in him, she wished the night would never end. She wasn't sure how this had happened, or why. She only knew that morning, with all its problems, was something she didn't want to see.

Yet, after hours of velvet oblivion that flew by all too quickly in their brief glory, morning did come. When a beam of sunlight struck Jane's eyelids she flinched and rolled over so that she could bury her face in the pillow. But at last she could no longer ignore the reality of the new day, and reluctantly her eyes opened.

Stephen's face was the first thing she saw. He was propped up on his elbow watching her, a solemn expression in his eyes. "You don't know how much I've been tempted to kiss you awake," he said. "Even after last night I'd like to make love to you all over again. But I think I'd better not."

"Why do you think that?"

"Because we have to talk. Last night was crazy and wonderful. But now we have to talk."

"Yes." She rolled over on her back and lay staring blindly up at the ceiling, knowing he was right. But though she'd just agreed to a discussion, she shrank from the thought of putting her worries into words. "You shouldn't have missed that cast party," she murmured. "The kids will have been disappointed that neither of us were there."

"That's right," he agreed evenly. "I feel bad about it, but there were more important things to attend to. And maybe today we can both do something to make amends."

Pushing aside the covers, he got out of bed and walked naked out into the living room. From there she heard him dial a number on her phone. "Hello, Alberta?" he said after a moment, and Jane marveled at how normal his voice sounded. No one would have guessed that after a night of stormy passion he was standing naked in her living room.

"This is your leader speaking." He chuckled at Alberta's retort and then continued apologetically, "Ms. Cowle and I both feel bad about missing the bash you guys threw last night. I wonder if we could get back into your good graces by taking you all to dinner at Hinckley's this evening?" he asked, naming a popular restaurant near campus. Stephen laughed again. "Well, I'm glad you're all so forgiving. Eats on me, of course, and endless beer for everyone who's legal."

A few minutes later he came back into the bedroom. "You heard what I told Alberta." He squinted at the clock on Jane's bedside table. "It's eight now. We have until seven this evening to work out all our problems."

Despite herself, her lips twitched. "Since we have some that are insurmountable, I think that might be rushing it a bit."

"We'll see about that. In the meantime, let's tackle the one at the head of the line." He sat down on the edge of the mattress. "I have no intention of leaving this apartment until we've settled things between us. But before we get started, I'd also like to shower and dress."

She was puzzled. "So?"

"So I don't want to have to climb back into that monkey suit I wore for the performance last night. Do you have something else I can put on?"

"Actually, I think I might." She started to get out from under the covers herself and then thought better of it. It might not bother Stephen to stroll around nude, but under the circumstances it would her. Pulling the sheet loose from its moorings, she wrapped it around herself toga style before leaving the bed.

Stephen watched this exercise in modesty with an impassive face. It wasn't until she'd knelt down in front of her bureau with her back to him that he said in a low, seductive voice, "Janie, I have every square inch of you memorized. If you were wearing steel armor, I could look right through it and see your breasts, the mole on your rib cage, the way your hips swell from your waist. My hands know the feel of your thighs as intimately as they know themselves. There's no way you can hide yourself from me, so you might as well not even try."

The words, spoken so quietly in his deep voice, made her insides feel weak. "There's more to a relationship than just the purely physical," she whispered.

"I know that as well as you. But, Jane, we have to start somewhere in this negotiating session. Will you admit that in bed we have everything going for us?"

Her head bent on her slender neck. "Yes." How could she not admit it? Last night they'd come together with the explosive force of an earthquake. Stephen was everything she could ever desire in a lover and more.

"Janie, do you have any idea how rare that kind of compatibility is?" he persisted. "Once you're lucky enough to find it, you're a fool to abandon it lightly."

"I think I understand that even better than you. After all, I spent five years in a sexually damaging marriage." She slid open the drawer and took out some folded material. Then she turned her head and looked back at him. "Now I feel embarrassed about giving this to you."

"What is it?"

With a little shake of her head, she rose to her feet and handed over what she'd unearthed. "It's something I bought as a joke. I was going to give it to you for Christmas, but after what happened when we got back from California, I decided not to."

He accepted the square of black jersey knit material she proffered and unfolded it. Then he started to laugh. "Very appropriate." It was a T-shirt with one very large word printed on the front: "ANIMAL."

"I just thought it was funny."

"It is funny." Grinning, he slung the shirt over his arm. "After I've washed up I'll wear it over my suit pants. Then we'll continue this discussion. Okay?"

"Okay."

Pausing, he eyed her questioningly. "Unless, of course, you'd like to join me in the shower?"

Irrationally, she was tempted to do just that. But now was not the time for that. She shook her head, and then watched as he sauntered out of the bedroom in the direction of the bath. When he'd closed the door behind him she stood for a moment and looked around. The bed was a shambles, testifying to the impetuous urgency of their night. Yet, though she certainly hadn't intended to make love to Stephen like that again, she couldn't regret it. Nor could she regret that he was here. Maybe he was right—it was better that they have this out once and for all.

Frowning as she pondered that, she changed into jeans and a white sweater, brushed her hair, and made the bed. Then she paused in front of her jewelry box. On impulse, she took out the silver chain with its small, delicately wrought pendant. Stephen hadn't made any reference to it, nor had she mentioned the little Christmas gift to him. Yet the message that had accompanied it seemed to say it all. Stephen wanted her to give herself to him in a way that just wasn't possible. She couldn't just abandon everything she'd worked toward and go to Hollywood with him.

Casting her now respectably neat bedroom a last cursory glance, she went out into the living room toward the kitchen. On the way she passed the broken mug with its spilled cocoa. Overnight the brown liquid had dried into a crusty stain, and she reflected that she'd probably have to buy a new carpet. After she'd started a pot of coffee on the stove, she went back out, picked up the remains of the mug, and tried to sponge away some of the cocoa. It wasn't long, however, before she gave up and returned to the kitchen to get the rest of her and Stephen's breakfast started. When he emerged from the bathroom she was in the middle of scrambling eggs and toasting English muffins.

"Smells great in here," he commented. Leaning against the doorjamb, he watched as she stirred the eggs. As far as Stephen was concerned, Jane was beautiful no matter what she had on. But, except for the way she looked naked in bed, he liked her best this way—wearing faded jeans that clung to her tidy little backside, her long hair down around her shoulders, and her face innocent of makeup and still pink from his kisses. He wanted to see her like this every morning for the rest of his life. And, he told himself, he was going to do his damndest to make sure that's how things turned out. She was his love, and losing her was simply unthinkable. But he also knew that he had to go carefully and not repeat any of the mistakes that had split them up in the first place. If only he could be sure of exactly what those had been.

Turning, she looked him up and down. "The shirt suits you."

"Do you really think so?" Making a comical face, he pretended to try and read the letters upside down. "Well, right now I feel like an animal," he admitted. "A hungry animal."

"Then sit yourself down. Breakfast is ready."

It was obvious that she was uptight about what was coming, so Stephen decided to wait until he was through with his eggs and muffins before starting his main attack. Why spoil his and Janie's first meal together in weeks with an argument? Instead, he tried to get her to relax by talking to her about other things—the food, the weather, some of the people he'd seen in the audience during last night's performance, and the complimentary comments he'd overheard them making. In an attempt to please her, he brought in the morning paper and read aloud a review of *Caitlin* that praised the opera and Jane's performance to the skies.

But none of that eased the guarded expression from her eyes. Indeed, the review seemed to wind her even tighter. When he looked up from the newsprint she was pushing her food around on her plate in a way that made him instantly decide to fold up the paper and put it away. After it was out of sight he changed the subject by asking about Carlie.

"Has she told you that she's reconciling with her ex-husband?"

"Yes. She talked to me about it Christmas Eve."

"What do you think?"

Frowning slightly, Jane started to spread jam on the last half of her muffin, more for something to do than because she was hungry. When Stephen had brought up the subject of Caitlin again, she'd lost her appetite. "Well, I don't know. They had a lot of problems to overcome."

"Yes, but she seems determined to make a go of it this time. Why, I wonder?" Casually, he got up to pour himself a second cup of coffee.

"I suppose it's because she's realized that she's in love with the man, and she doesn't want to go on living without him."

He turned toward her, his cup lifted only part of the way to his mouth, which was now set in a straight line. "Love. Do you think that makes it all worth the effort?"

"Maybe it does," she answered. Even before the words were out, her gaze locked with Stephen's, and she realized how she'd been maneuvered.

"Jane, tell me something," he asked softly. "Do you love me?"

Asked point-blank that way, she couldn't think how to avoid answering the question. And with his dark gaze holding hers prisoner, she couldn't lie. "Yes," she answered in a voice that was barely more than a whisper. "At least, I think so."

"Ah," he said. "You think you might love me, yet you were going to send me away without even telling me so."

"I didn't need to tell you. You knew it." It was a poor defense and Jane realized it.

He took a small sip of coffee. "Yes, I guess I did. You wouldn't have slept with me if you hadn't felt something. But it was nice to hear the words just now. I'd like to hear them over and over again. I'd like you to whisper them against my mouth when we're making love tonight."

She looked down at her plate. "Stephen, we're not going to—"

"Don't say it!" All at once there was an edge to his voice. "You're wrong. We will be in each other's arms tonight. First, though, there are a few things we have to get straight."

Jumping to her feet and looking everywhere but at him, Jane began to gather up the soiled dishes on the table.

"Jane, leave those things and come into the living room, where we can have this out in a civilized way."

Shaking her head stubbornly, she scraped the remnants of their breakfast into the garbage disposal. "Dried-on food is a mess to clean." She squirted liquid soap into the sink and began to run hot water over the plates and glasses. In less than ten minutes, however, there was nothing left to wash. When she started scrubbing at the already spotless countertops, Stephen lost patience. Removing the sponge fom her hand, he clamped authoritative fingers around her wrist and led her out into the living room. He made her sit on the couch. For several seconds he stood looking down at her.

"Why are you avoiding talking to me? If you were telling the truth back there and you really do love me, you should want to try and work through this problem we're having."

"I would if I thought there was a solution."

Baffled and frustrated by her attitude, he scratched his head. "All right, let's take it from the top. A little while ago you told me that there was more to a relationship than sex. Surely you don't think that what we have is mainly sexual?"

She twisted her hands together. "No. Though you have to admit that spending Thanksgiving weekend with you really got things started."

"Yes, but you would never have agreed to stay if there hadn't been more between us than physical attraction." His eyes narrowed speculatively. "In fact, for a long time we didn't have that. You never felt anything for me physically when we were undergraduates, did you?"

She looked up. It was true that ten years ago she'd never seen Stephen as a potential lover. She'd experienced some stirrings when he'd forced that kiss on her, but otherwise she'd been too infatuated with Ward to think of Stephen as anything but a friend. "What are you getting at?"

He knelt down in front of her and took her hands. "Don't you see? What we have physically is built on a very solid foundation. We were friends years before we were lovers. And we were friends because we had a lot in common—our interest in music, our way of seeing things, our laughter. There's no way you can say that what we have together is just some transitory sexual thing. The love we feel for each other is much more than that."

Jane stared at him helplessly. "Oh, Stephen . . ."

"The way we worked together on *Caitlin* proves that," he continued eagerly. "We made a great team. Jane, I don't think you know how good you were up on that stage. I couldn't take my eyes off you. You were . . . it was . . ."

He'd said the wrong thing, and her mood swung violently. "I know what's coming next," she flung at him. "You're going to tell me again that I *was* Caitlin. And I just don't think I can bear to hear it one more time." White-faced, her voice quivering with emotion, she folded her arms on her knees and bent her head.

Aghast, Stephen stared down at her shaking shoulders. "What's wrong? What have I said? Don't you want to hear how good you were?"

"No!" She lifted her head high enough so that she could glare at him. "I think if I hear another word about Caitlin, I'll scream. Why are you so blind? Don't you realize that it's her you love and not me at all?"

Stephen rocked back on his heels. "You can't be serious."

"I mean every word."

Stephen's breath hissed through his teeth. "I know you said something like this to me before, but I didn't take it seriously. Now I see that I should have." He took her face between his palms. "Do you really think I'm so crazy that I can't tell the difference between you and a character I've created for an opera?"

"Time and again you've told me that I *am* Caitlin."

"And so you are. But," he continued swiftly when he felt her go rigid, "only in a very narrow sense. Jane, ten years ago you saw me only as a friend. But I was in love with you. There was nothing mythical about you then. You were a real, flesh-and-blood girl with likes and dislikes and weakness and good points. But I loved you. Even though you hurt me, I continued to love you."

"You mean you continued to adore my memory, which is something very different."

"All right." His hands dropped away from her and he raked a hand through his tangled curls. "I admit that I may have made a sort of holy relic out of your memory. Maybe I wrote *Caitlin* because I needed to do something about that—exorcise it—I don't know."

"But instead of doing that, you came back here, found me, and persuaded me to sing the part," Jane pointed out with more than a touch of bitterness. "And now Caitlin and I will always be mixed up together in your mind!"

"No!" The denial was explosive. Seizing her hands this time, he jerked her toward him so that their faces were only inches apart. "When I first saw you and we had coffee together at Blake's, I had the same thought. That's why I didn't ask you out then, why I hung back for so many weeks. I'm no moon-struck kid. I'm an adult, Jane. I know my own mind. I finally realized that I wanted you—you the flesh-and-blood person, not some ghost from the past. It's you I love—and God, how I do love you! You can't look into my eyes and deny it. You know it's true!"

Fresh tears began to stream down her cheeks, and she couldn't say a word. With a groan, Stephen rose to his feet and pulled her up with him. Limply, she lay against his chest, her arms around his waist and her damp face pressed against the softness of his T-shirt.

"Do you believe me?" he asked.

It took a moment, but when she answered it was in the affirmative. "Yes. I believe you."

"And you never really did before?"

"Oh, I don't know. Sometimes I did. But sometimes I felt like someone going around in a disguise," she whispered brokenly, "and it was tearing me apart. I'm so far from perfect, and I've made so many mistakes. I thought that when you found out how human I was, you'd be disillusioned and wouldn't want me anymore."

Tenderly he stroked her hair. "I'll never stop wanting you. It's when you're being human that I love you the most—like last night," he added deeply.

Saying nothing, she quivered at the memory and her sobs gradually quieted.

"Is that what this was all about?" he asked finally. "Have we solved the problem?"

But they hadn't. There was much more to it. Slowly she shook her head and then drew away. "The Caitlin business doesn't make any difference, really. You're still going back to Hollywood, and I can't follow you there."

Stephen grimaced. "What you really mean is that you *won't* follow me."

"All right, I won't." She shot him a quick, pleading look. "Try to understand—"

"Jane, give me some credit. I do understand," he cut in. "You're happy here. You're succeeding on your own and you don't want to lose that in order to tag after me. It wouldn't make any difference if we were married, would it?"

Her eyes widened slightly, but after a moment she shook her head. "No. Marriage wouldn't make any difference. I've worked too long and too hard to be my own person. I can't give that up—not now."

"All right, I can understand that too. What I don't comprehend is why, if you love me, you aren't willing to try and work something out with me."

"What is there to work out?" she asked in a baffled tone.

Stephen looked exasperated. Pivoting, he rested his hands on his hips and took several brisk steps to the end of the room, then, checking abruptly, he once again turned toward her. "I've had an offer to produce my opera in New York. I've also been asked to become composer in residence here at Skyler."

Jane's heart began to flutter. "Do you mean that you might be willing to give up the movies in order to live here?"

"No," he said unequivocally. "I've worked long and hard to build my career too. I want to go on composing for the films."

She clasped her hands together tightly. Of course he wasn't going to abandon his success in Hollywood just to accommodate her. She'd seen for herself how much he liked it there, and she wouldn't want him to make such a sacrifice. It would only poison their feeling for each other. "Then I still don't understand what you mean."

"Jane, have you stopped to consider that we are in the last quarter of the twentieth century? I can be on either coast in a matter of hours."

"Surely you're not talking about living here and commuting to California."

"Not exactly, but with your cooperation something along those lines might be possible. Right now my career is in a period of transition. I don't yet intend to give up my film work, though it's possible that some time in the future I may opt to go in a different direction. For the present I'd like to keep my contacts alive here in the East. I'd like to see *Caitlin* produced in New York, and I wouldn't mind taking on a few special students here at Skyler from time to time."

Jane studied him anxiously. "Just what is it that you're proposing?"

He moved toward her, his face all at once a study in tenderness. "First of all, I'm proposing that you marry me." There was a pause while he waited for her reaction. When she only continued to stare at him, her blue eyes open very wide, he went on more briskly. "Second, I'm proposing that during the school year we live here at Skyler for however long that suits you." He waited again, but again she only continued to stare. Firmly he went on with what he intended to say. "I'll have to fly to the West Coast periodically, but most of my work is the kind I can take home with me, you know. I don't have to live next door to the studio to compose music."

In a faint voice, Jane finally managed a verbal response. "Oh, Stephen, you don't want to give up your beautiful house on the beach, do you?"

"No, I don't. I'd want us to spend our summers and vacations there, and any other time we could get away." Once more he paused, suddenly looking uncertain, his eyes questioning hers. "Do you think you could stand being that much a part of my life in Hollywood? I know you didn't enjoy that affair I dragged you to at Marsh Hughes's, but sometimes in my business social functions of that sort are unavoidable."

Feeling as if her heart were about to burst with new life, she flew across the rest of the distance that separated them and threw her arms around his neck. "Of course I could!" Lovingly, she stared up into his face. "Oh, Stephen, when you took me out to California, I was crazy about you. But I was also convinced that it couldn't be anything with us but a temporary fling. That colored the way I saw things. I reacted negatively to everything because I was really trying to prepare myself to lose you."

"That's never going to happen!" He shook his head and then buried his face in her hair. "Jane, I love you so much. I lost you once, but I'm never going to lose you again. Never!"

"No," she agreed, drawing his mouth down to

hers. And as their lips blended and her body melted into his, she knew for the first time that he was absolutely right. This time they'd really found each other, and they would never default on that sweet reprieve again.